D0775468

CHAMELEON

Also By Cidney Swanson

The Ripple Series
Rippler
Chameleon
Unfurl
Visible
Immutable
Knavery
Perilous

The Saving Mars Series
Saving Mars
Defying Mars
Losing Mars
Mars Burning
Striking Mars
Mars Rising

The Thief in Time Series
A Thief in Time
A Flight in Time
A Sword in Time
A Crown in Time

Books Not in a Series
Siren Spell

CHAMELEON

BOOK TWO IN THE RIPPLE SERIES

Cidney Swanson

For Natalie

Excerpted from My Father's Brilliant Journey, by Helga Gottlieb

Killing Kathryn Ruiz and her daughter Samantha seemed a simple assignment. My father could have given the task to any of his several assassins, but he chose Hans. The choice set off whispered speculations at Geneses' headquarters. "Who were they, the mother and child? Anyone important?" "Are they chameleons? I heard they were chameleons." "Does this child pose a special threat?"

The child, then seven, would indeed pose a threat; she was a latent as opposed to an actualized chameleon; and she was important, being descended directly from an important blood-line. These things my father knew, but he kept them to himself.

He'd given the assignment to Hans for a much less interesting reason: Kathryn Ruiz and her daughter lived in a small town. In Las Abuelitas, a new car or a new face could not hope to escape notice, and Hans knew how to keep a low profile. Not that his murders were hum-drum affairs—he had a fondness for gas leaks and consequent house fires where only the foundation remained. But he carried out his assignments such that investigations were never lengthy and often avoided entirely.

Hans began his task by purchasing the car of a man the townspeople considered a harmless drunkard. Hans spent a dull day hidden in Harold's car, observing the neighborhood, noting the Ruizes did not have a gas line.

When the mother and child drove up to the house, Hans heard a seven-year-old's squeal of pain or frustration and saw

1

something small scurry out the car, the girl following it into the street. The mother stepped out into the road as well. Because it was dusk, Hans couldn't be sure if the something small was a cat or a dog. The creature paid no heed to the calls from the little girl: a cat, most likely. Perhaps, in his mind's eye, Hans saw himself running the cat over with his new set of wheels.

This was the solution to his assignment. He started the engine.

Seeing no headlights, Kathryn at first thought the car she heard must be on an adjacent street. Then her ears warned her to clear the road. She grabbed the child at the elbow and pulled her to the sidewalk. But the little girl, intent upon her kitten, dashed back. Kathryn shouted and ran, intending to push the child out of danger. She failed.

By the time Hans collided with his twin targets, he noted he'd reached forty-five miles per hour. Hans always double-checked his work. He exited the car, raced invisibly towards the bleeding pair, checked quickly for one pulse and then the other. Satisfied that they were dead, Hans darted back to his waiting vehicle and drove off as curtains drew aside to reveal the faces of curious neighbors.

"Crazy Harold, driving too fast," they said. "Probably drunk again." The neighbors let their curtains fall shut, returning to their televisions and dinners.

Harold's drunken state when Hans found him again made it almost too simple. Hans drove out of town, Harold in the car beside him. An empty bottle of Jim Beam provided a nice bit of set dressing. Hans chose an especially sharp curve to send the *vehicle over the cliff. Locals called it Dead Man's Curve. He held the wheel straight and drove off the edge. Harold looked confused when Hans' body evaporated into the safety of nothingness.*

The invisible man smiled at the gratifying explosion.

(Note to self: Of course, Hans failed to kill Samantha, and my father later reversed his orders. Instead of wanting her dead, he wanted her alive: why?)

1

WINTER CHILL

I sat beside our pool gathering the last gasp of fall. Blowing past me in gusts, the air breathed November's chill, heavy with the sweet smoke of burning autumn leaves.

I'd returned the plate from my birthday cake to the bakery today. As soon as I'd walked inside, my ex-friend Gwyn had run behind the kitchen door.

It hurt.

I wiped tears from the corners of my eyes. The sky grew darker, threatened wintry rain, and I breathed in the melancholy passing of autumn.

Behind me, the sliding glass door opened, but I didn't turn. It had to be Sylvia, worried about me. But then I turned to see Gwyn, standing and holding papers in her hands, as if I had conjured her with my tears.

My hand rose self-consciously to the bruising upon my face, and I saw her lips draw tight and thin.

She dropped a piece of paper and the wind caught it. We chased it, darting along the deck towards Sylvia's garden. I trapped the paper with one foot, reached down to grab it, and handed it back to Gwyn.

"Actually, they're for you." She handed me the remainder of the pages.

As I took them, the wind gusted again and the pages flapped—frightened white birds trying to escape. I held them tight.

"I thought some of those might help Will. There's stuff for you, too." She looked at me and shook her head as she inspected my bruised face. "This is what a true friend does."

I dropped my eyes to the pages I held. Articles, printed off the internet. About how to recover from the compulsion to harm animals, how to leave an abusive relationship. I didn't know what to say. "Thanks" wasn't honest. I wanted to scream over the injustice of the situation. No words came.

"I'll be seeing you," said Gwyn. "But I can't be your friend until you give him up. It's not right and you know it."

She turned and walked away as I stood there, my throat swelling, eyes stinging. As I heard her car start, icy rain began to fall.

2

GENESES

Cross country finished for the season and I feared I'd see Will less, but we still had classes. We ate lunch together in the cafeteria where Gwyn cast dark looks at Will and avoided meeting my eye. Though we were around each other constantly, I couldn't figure out Will's feelings for me. At times, he seemed interested. A look captured as we ran together, his hand on my skin, resting a millisecond too long. I knew I should ask him. But how do you strike up that kind of conversation? *So, it's been awhile since we kissed . . . is there something you'd like to tell me?* I guess deep down, I knew it had been impulsive on his part and that he regretted it.

Or maybe he'd told his sister and she'd forbidden him from dating. As his legal guardian, Mickie had a lot of say in her brother's life. Anyway, our lives were complicated enough without throwing a relationship in the mix. Having the ability to turn invisible, or *ripple*, might sound pretty cool. And that was the problem: other people thought it sounded cool and wanted to capture or kill Will and myself because of our genetic abilities. We'd kept our skill secret from all outsiders and even my parents.

Mickie and Will had been in hiding ever since her former college advisor, the geneticist Dr. Pfeffer, had been murdered. A "witness protection thing minus the protection," Will called his life with his sister in Las Abuelitas, California. One of Pfeffer's last acts had been to secure the cabin for Will and his sister, bringing them to my home town last year.

I was supposed to be comforted by Will's reassurances that Dr. Pfeffer had left no trail linking Mickie to Pfeffer. He'd paid her in cash when she helped with research; he'd allowed no conversations by phone or even email; he'd insisted she disguise her appearance on her visits to his lab. If he had needed to send her anything, it had been done by regular mail, stuffed inside what appeared to be wedding invitations.

Of course, my life was in at least as much danger as either of theirs; last month we'd learned that Pfeffer's successors—and probable murderers—wanted me as well. The fact that they wanted me *alive* and not dead didn't comfort me.

We all felt eager for the French Club trip to France which would allow us, at last, to meet Pfeffer's trusted friend, Waldhart de Rocheforte, whom we jokingly referred to as Sir Walter. His letters had a decidedly chivalrous tone. Will and I would go on the trip as students; Will's sister would be a chaperone.

At school today, I carried the lunchtime conversation along without Will saying much. Something was really bugging him; his eyes kept glassing over, even in History—a subject he loved. As we walked into Biology, I brought it up.

"What's with you today?"

"Tell you after class."

I took notes on the circulatory system wondering what had him upset. He walked out with me after class dismissed.

"So?" I asked.

"We got another 'wedding invitation.' This one came with a video," he replied. "A disturbing video."

I frowned. Sir Walter continued the habit of his friend Pfeffer, sending information disguised in large, calligraphy-covered envelopes.

"Am I invited to come watch this disturbing video?" I asked.

"Mick wanted you to come over as soon as possible," he replied. "I couldn't sleep last night after we watched it."

We shoved Will's bike in the back of my Blazer and drove the two miles to Will and Mickie's shabby cabin, located just a mile down the highway from my own McMansion.

"Sam, thanks for coming so quickly," Mickie said, opening the door for me.

Will handed me the latest wedding invitation. "Read it. Then we'll watch the recording."

I looked at the familiar loopy handwriting of our mysterious contact in France.

Ma Chère Mlle Mackenzie,

Please allow of me to offer apologies for not responding sooner. Much has happened. Since I last wrote to you, I have been working upon plans which will slow, and I pray stop, those whom Pfeffer opposed.

Pfeffer told me before his death that he had located a manuscript—a small leather book, black. If he managed to pass it to you, guard it with your lives. The language would appear strange to you; it is obscure and little-spoken these days. Many lives might be saved by what it reveals about Helmann's dark activities.

I am most eager for our upcoming meeting.
Your friend and well-wisher,
Waldhart de Rochefort

Mickie completed a circuit around the room, closing blinds and curtains. On her computer, she typed through several password encryptions and the video began.

Intrigued, I watched images of war, poverty, starvation, and want in all its many faces from places around the globe while a deep-voiced, compassionate-sounding woman spoke of how desperate things had become for our planet. I was just deciding it was a commercial for a global relief project when a man drifted across the screen, dressed like Laurence of Arabia, or maybe Moses. He smiled as fountains of water blossomed across a desert land yielding row after row of crops. And as a farmer's daughter from central California, I can tell you that doesn't happen overnight. Someone had clearly designed the film to make impracticable tasks appear simple. The narrator switched to an urgent, hopeful tone calling on me to help bring this prosperous future into reality.

The image passed to a scene where happy, blond-haired, blue-eyed children sat on picnic blankets in a sunny garden, learning the multiplication tables and the periodic chart of elements. Interspersed were images of the children looking dreamily at a statue of the man who'd greened up the desert.

That's when I realized it was the film's music that really got you. This was music that should be played for astronauts soaring to infinity and beyond. Music to launch tall ships with broad sails. With music like this you could convince a person to do or dream anything.

Including a blondes-only future. I shivered, reminded of the black book. With the exception of dark-eyed "Pepper," the children in the black book had been fair and light-eyed.

I became distracted by memories of the awful things recorded in that book and only half-caught words the video punched.

PROSPEROUS . . . HARMONIOUS . . . WORTHY . . . FOLLOWERS . . . NEW ERA . . . THOUSAND YEARS . . .

The propaganda clip ended, cutting to a man standing behind a podium, emblazoned with the phrase "Geneses Corp Worldwide." The man looked ready to give a speech to the small gathering of crisply dressed business men and women.

"Imagine, if you will, a world without hunger." A dramatic pause. "A world without poverty or ignorance." Another dramatic pause. "A world without pollution, overpopulation, global warming, disease . . ." He paused even longer as the camera panned slowly across the small audience. "You will ask, 'how is it possible?'"

"How's it possible without killing off four billion innocent people," muttered Mickie.

"As with all visionary undertakings, we work for a future that will be enjoyed by our children and our children's children. There will be sacrifice—necessary sacrifice—made by our own generation in order to bring about this new world.

"But ask yourself, if there are none bold enough to take the steps we propose, what will the world of tomorrow look like? I need not spell this out for you." Behind him flashed images of disease, war, fetid water, and dying crops.

"The deaths of so many should indeed cause grave concern. And it is of grave concern to me, as I am sure it is to you. Yet, these souls will perish." Here he sighed deeply, gazing downwards and shaking his head as if with regret. "Whether by our hand or another's, they have, even the youngest of them, less than a century before they will be gone and forgotten." Another sad shake of the head. "Such a waste. And while they live their squalid existences of abject poverty and suffering, they continue to consume and destroy the very planet that gives them life."

More images of corpses and the dying, flies crawling along their diseased bodies.

"Who would prolong this level of suffering another hundred years, or another fifty, or even ten, when it lay in his power to put an end to it? To deliver mankind into the paradise for which he was intended by his creator?"

Here the music began to swell in quiet hopefulness.

"Once we have laid to rest the billions who consume and destroy, whose lives are but a daily torment even to themselves, we shall bring about a world without cripples or blindness, a world where no child lives in reach of the icy hand of cancer, where everyone has enough *and* enough time within which to enjoy it."

The music crescendoed; we were back to the launching-of-tall-ships overture.

The video ended before I could tell what the audience's response had been.

"What. Was. That?" I half-whispered the words, not sure I wanted an answer.

"We don't know," said Will.

"But this is a total game-changer from what I thought we were up against," said Mickie. "It's bigger than just killing off people with the gene for Helmann's Disease."

"Uh, yeah," I said. "If I understood correctly, that dude is discussing the need to sacrifice a generation of people living now so that his new world can happen. I'd guess Geneses isn't putting that on their website. They're the biotech company in San Francisco, right? The one fighting for a cure for cancer or something?"

"That's their public image," Will replied.

"So, guys, I'm lost," I said. "What does this video have to do with rippling or Helmann's Disease?"

"Oh, there's a connection." Mickie spoke softly. "Sir Walter labeled the video 'Helmann's Speech.'"

Letter from Helga Gottlieb to her father, circa present day

My Most Dear and Revered Father,

I write to explain an undertaking which I believe will at once please you and benefit mankind. I have begun these past several months to compile a collection of essays and stories which one day I hope to use to tell to all the world the story of your Accession to Greatness, and thus the story of the Salvation of Mankind through your Glorious Revitalization of the Earth in the near future.

As you know, I have in my care the journals compiled during the years of your youth and containing your earliest efforts at the Improvement of the Race of Man. Hans believes I should ask your blessing. However, I trust I have your permission as I sift through these thousands of entries to create a Biography of the Greatest Man ever to live, that is, your own illustrious self.

Believe me to be, Sir, your most obedient daughter and devoted servant,

Helga Gottlieb

3

BLACK BOOKS

I lay awake listening to the howling wind as it chased a snow-storm toward the Sierra Nevada mountains. Sleep felt as far away as summer right now. I shivered and dove farther under the covers as rain began pelting my window.

Helmann—as in some descendant of *the* black-book-writing-Helmann who tortured children in the name of science—had plans to bring about the end of the world as we knew it. Will and I had already discovered that there was a connection between Geneses and Dr. Helga Gottlieb, the scientist who had taken over the lab where Will's sister had secretly studied rippling with Dr. Pfeffer. Finding out that Helga was therefore connected to Helmann horrified me, but it wasn't a great surprise either. All the signs pointed to her being descended from either the children in the black book or Helmann or both.

But glimpsing the plans of these dreadful eugenicists on video? And knowing that some of them wanted me alive for some purpose of theirs? My mind recoiled.

The wind gusted against my windows, the screens rattling like dancing bones. I thought of my grandmother's home decorated for the *Dia de Los Muertos.*

This was going to be a long night.

Mickie said this wasn't a time to panic. Plus, for now, Sir Walter had directed us to continue laying low.

And that was hard, because, honestly, I thought we should turn the video over to the CIA or *Sixty Minutes* or something. But Sir Walter promised he had something better in mind. "A way to more thoroughly defeat this evil," he'd written.

But what if he didn't? What if he couldn't? What if this year, this month, brought an end to the world as we knew it? Did I want to survive the kind of apocalypse Helmann envisioned? Like a drowning man grasping at flotsam, I clung to one truth: I would fight this. I'd fight with everything I had, given the chance. And that meant waiting until we got to France and met up with Sir Walter.

I twisted in my sheets, alert to a sudden tattoo of rain pelting dad's pickup out front. Harsh, insistent, relentless, this storm—like our enemies. I listed the ones I knew by name: Helmann, Hans, Helga.

My mind returned, as it often did, to a stack of black, leather-bound books. Nearly a month ago, I'd invisibly followed a man who'd come to town asking questions about me. Hans, the stranger, had turned out to be Helga Gottlieb's brother. Not only had he been in the area to learn about me, he'd also stopped at his sister's lab at UC Merced to deliver those black books into her keeping. He'd been upset with himself for leaving them outside in his car. Helga had handled them like they were explosives. Or holy relics.

What was so significant about those black books? Were they as valuable as the one Sir Walter wanted from us? From what I'd seen, Pfeffer's black book recorded experiments Helmann had inflicted upon children in World War II Germany. Did the other books record similar atrocities? Would Sir Walter find them useful as well?

I hungered to hold those books within my hands.

Frowning, I remembered the rainbow of sticky-notes that had been attached to some of the books in Hans' car. They had my mother's middle name "Elisabeth" written upon them, spelled the same unusual way she spelled it. Hans had referred to me as "the descendent of Elisabeth" when he warned Helga against harming me. What was so special about my mother? Or about me?

Those books haunted me.

***

When I'd turned sixteen last month, Dad had handed me the keys to his old Blazer. It ran loud, burned oil, and lacked a CD player. It was painted a hideous burnt orange. I loved it. California law forbids the newly-licensed teen to drive friends, but Will and I had found a work-around. Each morning before school, I drove to Will's. Then we switched so that Will, who'd held his license over two years, could drive the two of us to school. Legally.

I missed our mornings pounding the pavement, but running with a school bag wasn't practical, and the sun rose later each morning so it was now pitch black during the time when Will and I had run last summer.

The morning following the storm, the sun seemed to have missed the memo about dawn altogether. I drove to Will's with my brights on, revving the ginormous engine in his driveway, my signal to Will each morning. He dashed out, slamming the cabin door. This was his signal to Mickie to get out of bed each day.

As he drove, I told him about the stack of black books and how they'd ruined my night's sleep.

"And you say they looked just like the book Mickie got from Dr. Pfeffer?" he asked.

"The same," I confirmed.

"I'd sure like to get a peek inside one of them," said Will.

"Me too."

"I wonder where Helga's keeping them."

"Assuming she still has them," I said.

"It's just, if Sir Walter thinks *one* black book could be useful, then maybe *several* black books would be even more useful."

I squirmed. Now that Will spoke it aloud, the idea of retrieving additional books sounded very, very bad.

Distracted, Will hit the bad pothole on Main.

"Hey, respect the ride," I said.

"Dude, I *love* the ride," Will replied. "I want to *marry* the ride so it can have my children."

"Shut up," I chortled.

Gwyn emerged from Las ABC to my right. She glared at me, angry, and we both turned our heads quickly away from one another. But as Will slowed to turn into the school parking lot, I looked back one last time. Slowly, deliberately, Gwyn shook her head at me, frustrated that I seemed determined to remain with Will. It was so unfair, having to leave Gwyn's friendship behind so that I could keep Will's secrets. I turned away from my former friend, resting my head on the window.

It took effort to bring myself back into the present, to walk away from my regrets.

After a moment's silence I spoke. "No way can we go back there and get the books."

Will shrugged.

"Will, I mean it. Helga is dangerous. And crazy."

Will's mouth pulled into a frown as he eased the Blazer into a parking spot. "I've already been there, you know. Nothing bad happened."

I nodded. Will and Mickie had almost left Las Abuelitas for good last month when I'd described my encounter with Helga at UC Merced. Mickie had been scared to stay after that. But on their way out of town, they'd crashed their car. While his sister got stitched up and rested under medication, Will had snuck off to Helga's lab to see what he could learn.

"I've thought about going back to UC Merced a couple times," Will said.

"It would be such a bad idea," I said.

"Really bad."

So why did I get the feeling he was already planning a second trip?

I worried about it through Madame Evans' description of the Parisian *Métro* subway system. I worried about it as Gwyn glared at us from across the lunchroom. I worried about it while scrawling answers to a biology quiz.

Will met me at my Blazer after school. "So when do you think we should go?"

He must have been thinking about this all day just like me.

"Your sister will *never* let you do this," I said, slamming the passenger door shut.

"You're one-hundred-percent about that," said Will. "Which is why I'm thinking this Wednesday. She's going to a concert in Fresno."

"Of course she is," I said, resting my head on the window. Outside heavy clouds wafted across the wintry sky. "Let me guess: you just bought the tickets?"

Will guffawed. "No, but that's a great idea for the next time I want to do something she'd disapprove." Will leaned over to fist-bump my shoulder, and the car swerved across the yellow line.

"You!" I said, shoving him back. "Focus on steering straight."

Will placed his hands at 10:00 and 2:00.

I groaned. "So what's your plan?"

Excerpted from the private journal of Helga Gottlieb, circa present day

Within the pages of his journals, I seek the secrets my father still withholds from me. Why the repeated problems with the offspring I breed? I am certain Father has already discovered the answers I seek. He keeps these secrets to himself for what reason? Am I not the one scientist who could assist him in his Glorious Goals for the Improvement of Man?

My brother Fritz is nothing compared to me. A dabbler. Has Fritz dared to create life upon the principles we follow? Bah. He is a coward. An amateur. Alone of Father's children, I have parented a new generation. And with the dispassion required of a true follower of Science, I have eliminated those who proved inferior—so many failed attempts to bring into being the New Humanity. Yes, I denied the beating heart of the mother within me, rather than let inferior beings live.

And yet Father will not tell me what I am sure he knows.

Nor can I find anything within these volumes that I did not learn long decades ago studying alone in my laboratories.

I am determined. I will learn how to eliminate the flaws within my own offspring. I will create the New Humanity.

4

HELGA'S LAB

Wednesday night arrived. We'd decided to run to UCM since we didn't want anyone recognizing and tracing my Blazer. And so, on a dark November night, less than three weeks from our trip to France, we met at Will's cabin to execute our heist.

I had come up with an idea that I thought slightly brilliant. "I'll wear a double layer of black pantyhose over my face," I said. "In case Helga has set up cameras or something."

"You're making a big assumption," said Will.

"It just seemed like the kind of thing she *might* do."

"That's not the assumption I mean," said Will. "You're assuming I'm going to let you show your face in her lab."

"Will, I'm being completely logical. She's never seen you. She doesn't know you exist. It's important that we keep it that way." I paused before playing my ace. "Your sister's safety is hanging in the balance, too."

He scowled at me. "Fine. You get to be the one who grabs the books. But I don't like it. And I'm wearing the pantyhose hat, too," he said. "Just in case."

I examined his expression, dark and determined. "Fair enough. But you have to find your own pair." I grinned, certain this was something his sister wouldn't have lying around.

"Mick got some once for an interview," said Will, undaunted. "Hope they're still in her drawer." He rippled and I heard him rummaging in his sister's room, opening a drawer and slamming it shut.

He reappeared a moment later, nylons in hand, a silly grin on his face.

"How do you know what's in your sister's underwear drawer?" I blurted out before thinking.

Will flushed dark red and mumbled that they traded off doing laundry depending on who was busier.

"Oh," I said. Sylvia did all my laundry except cross country clothes; I was too mortified by eau-de-Sam to let anyone else near those. Will and his sister didn't have the luxury of being self-conscious.

I felt awful for embarrassing him, but he shook it off.

"I thought of something else," he said, rippling away again. When he solidified beside me a minute later, he revealed a pair of headlamps: the kind that strap around your head to light your way in the dark.

"Hands-free," he said, smiling. "Plus, in case you're right about cameras, I figure a light above your face would mess up any pictures."

"Genius," I said, nodding in admiration.

We adjusted the face-smooshing nylons and strapped the headlamps on. Will leaned in to flick mine on. I felt his breath warm against my polyestered face.

"The disguise really works—you're hideous," I said. "How do I look?"

Misshapen lips formed a lumpy smile on Will's face. "I would never pass judgment on a woman's appearance."

I shook my head, but it was true that I'd never heard him say anything about how a girl looked. "Your sister trained you well."

"We ready?" asked Will.

I nodded.

"I've been thinking we should hold hands," Will murmured. "So we don't lose track of each other."

Now it was my turn for a scarlet face. I hoped the dark nylons concealed this from Will. "Good thinking," I said.

"I'm pretty sure holding hands'll work," he said. "I mean, when you hold something while you're invisible, it stays in your hand unless you decide to drop it."

"Right," I agreed. Will's hand felt warm, callused, and like it belonged there, folded around mine. I felt my heart pounding faster. How could this boy go from a friend I joked with to someone who changed the rhythm of my pulse?

What if we could read one another's minds like before? *Crap!* This was not the kind of thing I needed to be thinking if we were about to turn invisible. Of course, it hadn't been "mind-reading" per-se, more like sharing images. This sounded more manageable. I just needed to avoid forming images of Will holding my hand or kissing me or . . . *Stop!* I told myself.

"We can totally do this, Sam," said Will, noticing my hesitation. "The running together part, it'll be just like cross country again, right? Except a lot faster. And without bodies." He gave my hand a quick squeeze and with that he vanished.

Will's hand in mine felt like ice now that he'd rippled. I tried not to see it as a metaphor for our relationship. But his heart simply didn't warm to mine.

Will came solid beside me again. "You sure you're ready?" he asked.

"I'm fine," I said. "As long as you stop interrupting my *process* here." I reached out an arm to

28

push him aside, but he rippled and was gone. I grunted out a single laugh.

Besides my aching heart, my mind circled around one other thing: fear of Helga Gottlieb. Not helpful. I needed to be thinking calm thoughts. Coach drilled us about visualizing success when we raced. So I imagined Will and myself succeeding in our lab break-in. I pictured us together in Helga's laboratory full of beakers, DNA strand drawings on the whiteboard . . . stacks of black books which we would steal. I felt a temperature change which meant I'd slipped out of my skin.

Together, Will and I took off running into the night, a cloudy sky pressing heavily upon the town. Las Abuelitas lay in the clutches of a winter's night: dead and brown and icy-still. Strange to run so silently, so swiftly alongside the empty road.

I could feel Will beside me, his presence far more real than I'd expected. At first, I seemed to catch nothing from his mind. But then I noticed I could see the road as he saw it, super-imposed upon what my own vision registered. The doubled vision should have baffled and disoriented me. But it didn't. My mind accepted both images.

Something from Will's mind flashed into mine; he'd spotted a pair of raccoons shambling alongside the road, their eyes fixed upon his invisible form as he passed. Animals sensed us, somehow. I wanted to communicate to him I'd seen what he showed me. Only I had no idea how to do this.

And now a thought flashed through me, white-hot like lightning: we had no way to talk to each other in Helga's lab.

Our inability to talk gnawed its way along my stomach. We should have thought about this. Would it endanger us in Dr. Gottlieb's lab, the silence that lay between us? I wanted to ask Will's opinion. Slipping my hand from his, I came solid.

Will rippled in front of me, sensing my absence. "What's wrong?" he asked, walking back to me.

"We won't be able to talk in the lab. Not while we're invisible. What if we need to say something to each other?"

Will frowned. "Hmmm. Let's get off the road."

We stepped into straggling grass that lined the highway and stopped beside the up-tilted slates, so like tomb-markers, scattered across the land in this area. In the dark, I couldn't make out the red lichen which had reminded me of bloodstains last October. Maybe the red lichen died back in winter. Will sat, slumping against one of the stone slabs. I squatted, avoiding the eerie standing slates.

"Man, it's cold." He looked at me funny. "Sit closer? For warmth?"

Self-consciously, I scooted closer. A small heat hummed between our bodies.

"Much better!" Will said, grinning.

He viewed me as a heat-source. Nothing more.

I shook back disappointment, let it float off on the cold night wind.

"I don't know if we'll need to talk. It's just, once I realized that we wouldn't be able to, I couldn't stop thinking about it," I said.

"Like a piece of popcorn-skin stuck between your teeth," he said.

I grunted out a small laugh.

"We both know what we're going in for, right?" Will asked.

"Duh."

"So, as long as nothing goes wrong, I don't know that we'd need to talk."

"Maybe," I said, trying to imagine what we might need to say to one another, picturing the lab again. "Omigosh! Will, I have an idea!"

He turned toward me, brown eyes curious.

"What if we imagined blackboards and visualized writing things on them?"

"Ni-ice," said Will, elongating the word into two syllables. "You're a genius!"

"Do you think it'll work?"

Will shrugged and stood. "Let's find out. It's too damn cold to sit here any longer." He reached for my hand, pulling me up. He started to let go once I'd arisen, then grasped again, mumbling, "Guess we need to hold hands."

He slipped into cool nothingness, and I turned my thoughts to the creek at Illilouette, the beauty of the clear water as it glided over multi-colored rocks. I rippled.

Immediately, in my mind's eye, I saw writing upon a chalkboard: *So this moose walks into a bar . . .*

I wrote on the board, *I see what you're writing!*

Letters formed like magic below mine, in Will's familiar writing. *So I think this works, huh?*

This is, like, a major scientific breakthrough! I wrote.

Which makes you a scientific genius, Will wrote back.

I smiled. *We could tell Mickie it was your idea, and she'd have to treat you with a little more respect, huh?*

Ha! Like that would ever happen, wrote Will. *But, seriously, Sam, no way are we ever telling her about tonight, okay?*

Will had a point. If we told Mickie about our discovery, it had to be minus the part where we visited Dr. Evil's laboratory.

I promise, I wrote.

Will wrote, *Pinky-swear?*

Guys don't pinky-swear, I wrote. *That's a girl thing.*

I was raised by a girl. Ish.

Fine. I pinky-swear, I wrote. *Now are we going to do this thing or what?*

Let's go!

Will and I tore off through the grass, back to the highway, gliding along at a speed that should have been terrifying but wasn't.

Birds must feel this way when they soar, I wrote.

It's like nothing else I know, wrote Will.

The silence felt eerie; normal running created all kinds of noise. Here we sailed with only the sounds of the night: an owl hooting, the rustle of grass in a breeze, the occasional whoosh of a car. We continued silent as the night creatures we passed along the highway to Merced. I could see an eerie glow from the city now, reflecting back down from the clouds. Merced used fog-lights designed to pierce the thick tule fog of winter. The orange-yellow light seemed to whisper, *Caution! Caution!* as we approached.

Check. This. Out. Will's handwriting appeared in entire words this time, instead of letter-by-letter.

Do you see what I'm doing now? Will asked. *I'm imagining whole words onto the board instead of spelling them out.*

I imagined myself writing out whole words at once. *Much faster this way.*

Too bad you don't know sign language, Will wrote. *I'm sure I can sign faster than I can imagine words on a chalkboard.*

That gave me an idea. *It doesn't have to be a chalkboard. We could write on a piece of paper.*

Or a computer screen—Will typed on an imagined screen and I saw it.

We can write on anything! The idea tickled me. This was stupid-fun.

We continued along the highway, experimenting within our shared mind-space.

My fastest method for sending thoughts was via an imagined cell-phone screen whereas Will's was on a blank piece of notepad paper. Will wrote that he'd always had a soft spot for pencils and notepads.

Far sooner than made rational sense, Will and I left the foothill country for the smooth floor of the Central Valley. UCM glowed at the outskirts of the town of Merced, and we aimed for it like moths drawn to a flickering flame.

I swallowed, praying for a better fate than that of the moth.

Will wrote to me, *Not exactly your most hopeful image, that last one.*

Yeah, sorry.

We're going to be just fine, wrote Will. *We get in, we find the books, we get out. You're getting better at rippling, you know.*

Thanks, I typed back. *I'm fine as long as nothing scares me.*

So we'll just avoid scary situations, wrote Will. Then he drew a huge smiley-faced sunshine on a clean sheet of paper and what I could only assume was a rainbow. It was very ugly.

Thanks, I typed.

He drew an arrow to the smiley and wrote *Sam* beside the arrow.

I felt laughter burbling inside me. Will knew how to make me lighten up.

Upon reaching the building that housed Helga's lab, I felt another mental shudder, remembering how Helga strapped me down to her dentist-chair in order to interrogate me. Will must have seen the image.

You know that's not happening this time, right? he wrote.

I know.

We're going to stick together, and besides, we're invisible, wrote Will.

Only until we grab the black books, I typed.

Good point, Will responded. *But no unnecessary risks. You risked a lot last time. Come on. Let me be the one who ripples solid to grab the books.*

Helga's never seen you, and *we need to keep it that way. This is about your sister, too, Will.*

He didn't write back immediately. *Alright. It's you that grabs the books. But if anyone at all is in the building, the whole deal is off, okay?*

Totally, I typed, wondering if we were idiots for doing this.

Excerpted from the private journal of Helga Gottlieb, circa present day

I have stolen the truth from Father's journals at last! A small fact which my father has chosen to keep from me these many years. Father believes the genes of the female de Rochefort line are superior to my own. Superior to his, that is, since I am his offspring. Well, if he can swallow this bitter knowledge, then so can I.

I do not know whether to be furious that Father would hide such information from me or to admire him for doing exactly what I, in his place, would have done.

But no. That is inaccurate. I know my feelings well enough at this moment. I am angry at this betrayal. How many times has Father praised my efforts in unlocking the hidden secrets of Nature's code, while, all the time, he knew me to be chasing down blind alleys?

But at last I hold in my hands this fact I have sought after for so long; I can accept it or reject it, but it will remain the singular truth: the very genetic sequences that have made my mind capable of so much more than the brightest minds Science has produced also contain sequences for psychoses. Not from my genes will the future salvation of mankind be created. But I shall not become embittered. I have not been defeated.

See? I write dispassionately. I can embrace truth and overcome it. Yes, I shall overcome this bitter discovery. And in this ability of mine to embrace what is, from that ability shall come triumph and the Improvement of the Race of Man.

Father bides his time, waiting to collect the genes of the girl descended from Elisabeth. I shall seize the opportunity. And the girl. Oh, yes, the girl. She will be mine before she becomes his!

5

WANTED

Here goes, I wrote as we bore down upon the front of the building.

Hey, Sam? No matter what, don't drop hands, okay? We can't talk if we aren't touching.

Right, I typed back. *I'm not letting go for anything.* If I let go, I had no idea how we'd find each other again, short of one of us coming solid.

We approached a large glass wall rather than using the building's front doors. Even though Will didn't write it out, I knew where he wanted to go. I'd have to ask him about it later. When we weren't trying to break into the high-security facility of a woman who was crazy or wanted me dead or both.

Together we passed into the viscous embrace of the large wall of glass. It felt just like I remembered from other times. Moving through glass warmed and calmed you. Like placing cold hands in a basin of tepid water. Like a hug from Sylvia. Like Will's lips on mine.

I tucked the last thought away, hoping Will felt distracted by the sensation of slipping through the glass. Gently, the window released us back into the air of the building's interior.

How do we both know where we're going? Will asked.

I don't know. It's weird, I replied.

Maybe it's 'cause we can see with each other's eyes when we're connected like this. Like, I see your eyes focusing on a particular corridor, and mine follow suit, and then that's just where it feels right to go, he wrote.

Turn off your inner-scientist, Will. Let's get this done.

I was seeing flashes from my previous incarceration. I didn't feel exactly scared by it, but it wasn't pleasant, either. *Don't worry, I'm fine,* I typed to Will. *Just remembering.*

It's nearly impossible to feel scared when you're invisible, Will wrote. *I made a few . . . errors of judgment coming solid in front of my dad because of how invincible I felt.*

Arriving, we paused in front of Dr. Gottlieb's laboratory.

Ready? asked Will.

Together we passed through the sawdust-dryness of her wood-veneered door. I understood now what flour felt like, coursing through a sieve. The lab lay in near darkness. Emergency exit signs and computer lights glowed and created an eerie range of Christmas-colored lighting throughout the room.

Let's start in her office, I wrote.

Hand in hand, we glided across the laboratory floor, our pace now slowed to an ordinary walk. We paused at the office door for half a second, and then sifted through. Another mouthful of sawdust-dryness.

Jackpot! wrote Will, directing his gaze to a bank-style vault behind her desk that ran from floor to ceiling. *That should be interesting to pass through.*

It was thicker than a regular door. A metallic flavor coursed through my nose and mouth as we slipped through. I pushed back ugly memories of my mouth, full of blood, of Helga's henchman poised to strike once more.

As we tried to pass to the far side of the vault door, we discovered something frustrating. Immediately behind the door sat shelves that extended to the door. Without any illumination, we could still sense the solid masses of shelving. Beyond the shelves the back wall of the vault pressed, followed by the outer wall of the building. Each time we tried to walk through to an area where we could stand and solidify, we found ourselves outside under the cloudy night sky.

This sucks, wrote Will.

No matter how hard we tried to find a "room" behind the vaulted door, we couldn't. Eventually we admitted what we knew: there was no "room," only shelving. We couldn't solidify inside the vault. On our third pass back through the vault, I recognized two scents besides the metallic flavor of the door. These odors were subtle compared to the strong tang of metal.

Paper, Will. That's the smell of old paper that's been somewhere damp. I thought of a visit to my grandma's house when I was little. Her books had smelled this way. I tried to place the other scent. It reminded me of my grandfather. *Leather!* I wrote. *I smell something like old, worn leather.*

The combined smells, paper and leather, conjured happy memories. Trips to the library, my mom and later my dad reading to me, the smell and feel of my grandparents' books. It was hard to reconcile such bright thoughts with what probably lay inside the pages of these black books.

I'm not smelling anything I recognize, Will wrote. *But paper and leather sounds like the journals. They must be here in the vault with us.*

I'm afraid so, I responded.

Damn. No way can we come solid in here.

We re-entered Helga's office and stood forlorn.

What's that? asked Will, his attention pulling mine to a picture drawn on a sheet of paper. *Is that supposed to be you?*

41

I stared curiously at the paper upon Helga's desk. Below the hand-drawn picture, done up like a "WANTED" poster, I read these words:

DO YOU KNOW THIS STUDENT? I HAVE HER PURSE.

A phone number was listed below the words. An orange sticky-note had been attached as well, reading "Apprehend, but Do Not Harm." The word "not" had been underlined several times.

She's trying to find you, said Will.

Looks like it.

At least she still believes you're a student here, wrote Will. *That's better than if she figured out that Samantha Ruiz was here.*

My eyes riveted upon something even more interesting. Lying open on the left-hand side of her desk sat a single black journal.

They're not all in the vault! I wrote.

Together, we stared at the innocent-looking book, a match to the book from Dr. Pfeffer.

Still written in gobble-de-gook? Will asked.

Looks like it, I replied.

Shall we? wrote Will, and I knew he wanted me to ripple solid and grab the book.

I want to check if there's anything else of value first.

He wrote back, *Good idea.*

We circled the office, noting a stack of the flyers with my likeness drawn upon them. We didn't uncover any other black books.

Guess this is it, then, wrote Will. *You sure it has to be you that grabs the book?*

I'm sure, Will. I'm not endangering you and Mickie in case there are hidden cameras.

Okay, then. I've seen enough of this place. Grab it and let's go, Will wrote.

It wouldn't be accurate to say that I "felt" Will dropping my hand, but I certainly sensed it. I pulled my hand towards myself and moved to the side of the desk where the book lay. Then I rippled solid, my headlamp illumining the room. As I reached for the book, I hoped Will was staying put so that I could find him again.

The leather cover felt cool against my palms. Time to ripple. I turned my thoughts to visions of still water. To one side, a fluttering motion caught my attention. Someone was rippling solid.

Someone besides Will.

6

IVANOVICH

A familiar voice ripped through the quiet of the office.

"What the hell are you doing here?" demanded a large man with ice-blue eyes.

I knew him. Helga's thug, Ivanovich.

"Did Dr. Helmann send you?" he asked, his visage aflame with anger or madness: I couldn't tell which.

I didn't speak. I felt like an insect pinned down by his glare.

"Turn off that damn headlight," he growled.

Not a chance, I thought.

"Who are you?" he asked, voice lowering to a less threatening tone. "Put that book down and let's talk."

He circled the desk and I circled too, keeping the same distance between us. I felt a blast of icy-cold that had to be Will. *Stay hidden*, I thought.

The blue-eyed man spoke again. "I said put that book down. Now!"

I clutched it more tightly to myself as I tried to reason my way out of this situation. I needed to ripple or run away. Or beat this guy up so bad that he couldn't come after me. The last one wasn't looking too likely.

As we continued circling the desk, the man pulled a knife from his jacket.

"I'll carve you into little pieces, girl. I don't care if Helmann *did* send you." Ivanovich's voice dropped. "He's not my boss. I serve only *her*."

"You're Helga's . . . creature," I said, still circling around her desk.

This seemed to please him. Blue-eyed man stopped circling and grinned, his lips stretching farther and farther until I could see all of his perfect white teeth. It was not a smile. It was feral. Dangerous.

"I'm the fore-runner of the new generation," he said, stalking me again.

I moved towards the door leading to the larger lab room. The door was closed. I yanked it open and then pulled it tight shut behind me. I ran for a door, but disoriented, I chose the small room where Helga liked to pull teeth. Behind me, I heard the office door open.

"Give me the book and I'll kill you quickly," said Ivanovich.

"You're crazy," I said.

"Crazy is not a designation that has meaning for the *übermensch*."

I dashed for the door that led out of the lab. Maybe I could hide in the ladies room I'd found last time: hide and ripple. As I wrenched the door open, my ankle gave way and I stumbled. A knife whizzed past me, through the space my head had occupied a moment ago.

A scream escaped me and I flew down the corridor, hurling myself around the corner.

"You're making this fun for me," called my pursuer. "I'll give you that." His voice followed me from behind. I heard him pause and imagined him recovering the knife.

I rounded another corner, hearing feet picking up speed behind me. No escape; no place to hide. I threw myself down a new corridor and felt an icy patch of cold air.

Will! I bit my tongue, keeping myself from saying his name aloud. Ahead, I saw a men's room.

"In there," whispered Will as he rippled solid. "I'll take him off your trail!"

Quick and silent, I slipped into the men's restroom. Beyond the door, I heard Will's footsteps continue down the hall. A moment later my pursuer found him.

"Another one?" roared Ivanovich.

My heart pounding, I crossed to the sink and started the water running. *Calm. Peaceful.* I stared at my hands, but they remained agonizingly solid. *Please.* And then I realized I didn't have the black book any more. I'd dropped it! I thought back through the last ninety seconds and realized it must have slipped from my grasp when my ankle tweaked. It was lying back beside Helga's lab door.

I almost dashed out the door to retrieve the book, but stopped myself: I needed to ripple first. Returning my gaze to the water, I thought of Will, racing down the hall to save my butt. Again. Like the night he'd drawn the police off my trail by Las ABC. I owed that boy; I was not letting Helga's thug hurt him. I turned off the water and closed my eyes, remembering Will's arms around me the day he'd kissed me. His lips on mine, cracked on one side, but soft and warm and . . . I'd rippled.

Gliding invisibly from the men's room, I retraced my steps. The corridors looked so similar to one another and I wasn't at all sure I was even going the right direction, but then I saw the black book, bent over upon itself half-way down the corridor to my left. I raced toward it and came solid again, leaning down.

A knife whirred past me for the second time. "Enough with the knives!" I shouted, dashing forward to make sure I got to the dropped weapon first.

At the far end of the hall, my pursuer paused. "How many of you did Helmann send?" he asked.

"You're being tested," I lied, wildly. "He sent a dozen of us to see how you'd stand up to us."

Ivanovich slowed his advance towards me, tilting his head to one side, considering me.

"And, you're doing really well," I said. "But he wants this book back now, so I'll just be going."

He bared his teeth once again. "You're lying. I can smell your fear."

"You don't smell so great yourself," I said, slipping the black book into my waistband and gripping the knife out in front of me, trying to look scary.

He laughed. He looked insane as he launched himself at me from down the corridor.

Suddenly Will solidified running alongside Ivanovich.

"Will!" I screamed.

Ivanovich caught Will's motion from the side and turned, taking a swipe at Will with yet another knife. Will rippled. I turned to flee, but then I heard Will yelling and spun back around. The two wrestled in a strange fashion, Will moving in and out of solidity. Helga's thug screamed his rage as Will took longer than usual to come solid.

"I can play at that game, coward!" he shouted. Then he vanished.

I took off, sprinting down the slippery corridor once more, and nearly barreled into the chest of *über*-man who had materialized directly in front of me. Terrified, I dropped his knife and twisted to fly the other way.

Again I collided into a body as it solidified in my path.

"No!" I cried, struggling within a grip cold and hard as iron.

7

ÜBERMENSCH

My struggles against this pursuer proved useless; maybe he couldn't even feel pain. I saw my form wavering along with his and despair overwhelmed me. *Ivanovich is rippling, taking me with him.*

But then as I vanished into nothingness, I smelled Will: clean-soap and pine-needles. Just who had grabbed me?

Sam, I got you. It's okay, wrote Will.

I recognized Will's yellow note-pad and his handwriting upon it, and I wanted to cry and laugh and run until we caught up to the sun.

Let's get out of here, I wrote on my imagined cell-phone screen.

Behind us, as Will and I slipped free, we heard the blue-eyed man howl his rage like a crazed beast.

The return journey passed in a blur. Will ran swiftly, overtaking cars as he "carried" me back to Las Abuelitas. We reached his cabin and drifted through the worn log-walls. Once there, I felt the moment when his arms slipped away from my form. After he came solid, I rippled back as well.

Will's ridiculous pantyhose-covered face was the first thing I saw, and it put a smile back on my face. I pulled off my disguise and gazed at the black book we'd risked so much to obtain.

"We did it," said Will, grinning.

I nodded, fretting over what exactly we had done.

"Don't look so worried," he said. "There's no way anyone could recognize us thanks to these." He held up the nylons and shot them across the room like a rubber band.

The pantyhose hit the living room pendant light and circled once before coming to a rest, bathing the room in a glow of "Nearly-Nude."

"Hmm," Will murmured, inclining his head as if in appreciation of the new décor.

"Get those down," I said, a small snort of a laugh escaping.

Will looked at me, eyebrows and hands raised in a "but, why?" gesture.

"Your sister, dweeb?"

Will rose, sighing in dejection. Grabbing the hose, he rippled, coming solid a half-second later, minus the incriminating evidence.

"Totally handy how we can make stuff disappear, huh?" asked Will.

I frowned. "I wonder if Ivanovich was planning to ripple away with me."

"I thought of that," Will said. "It's what gave me the idea."

"Thanks, by the way."

"I just hope I didn't give him a brand new idea he didn't already know about," said Will.

I thought for a moment. "You taking me away like that, it wouldn't look any different than if we'd decided to ripple at the same time, right?"

Will scuffed his shoe against the leg of his sister's desk. "Except for you were kind of kicking and fighting."

I felt heat rising to my face. "Sorry about that," I mumbled.

"So he probably had a pretty good idea of what went down," said Will. "Or he will have figured it out by now, being an *übermensch* and all."

"What's an *über*-whatsit?"

"It's an idea this philosopher Nietzsche had, about a new race of man who would transcend common man."

"Sounds right up Geneses' alley." A chill ran along my spine, stiffening the hairs on the back of my neck as I remembered Helmann's speech on the video.

Will scowled. "Yeah, pretty much. Among other things, the *übermensch* holds himself apart from common ideas of morality."

"Uh, yeah, I kind of got that when the knives started flying."

Will grunted a single laugh.

"Where do you get all this . . . stuff, you know, Shakespeare and Nietzsche and all?" I asked.

Will's face flushed. "There was this year after Mom died when Mick was supposed to be homeschooling me—I refused to go to school—only her idea of homeschool was to let me read anything I wanted and listen while I spouted over dinner."

"Wow."

"Yeah. Actually I don't know if she really listened—I'm the history-geek in the family—but she didn't make me shut up."

I struggled to recall a quote I'd heard my dad repeat. "Those who don't remember history . . . are . . . screwed. Right?"

Will laughed. "Close enough. So let's check out our ill-gotten gains, huh?"

The book in my hands felt smooth, the leather worn by many years of handling. "It's older than the other one," I said, holding it up for Will's inspection.

"You want to take this to your home and try translating?" he asked.

"Absolutely," I replied. "But what do we tell your sister about this book?"

Will pulled one hand through his tangle of curls. "I'm thinking she doesn't need to know about this at the moment. I mean, we don't even know what's inside yet, right? We can always tell her later, if it turns out to be important."

I swallowed, relieved. I didn't want to recount our evening's activities to Will's paranoid sister. "Do you think we're in any increased danger? Now that Ivanovich knows we both ripple?"

Will shrugged. "He seemed to think we were sent by Helmann." His mouth curved upward. "And trust me—you looked *nothing* like yourself with that disguise. Seriously, you looked like an alien being."

"Shut up," I said. But I laughed.

"Anyway," said Will, his face sobering, "We've got one more weapon in our arsenal. I bet Sir Walter will be very glad to see this book, whatever it contains."

We said goodnight. Driving the short mile to my home, I felt my heart thrumming with the memory of Will's hand touching mine. Why couldn't he see how right we were together? I ran the back of my sleeve across wet eyes. Within the bright tunnel of my head beams, tiny snowflakes drifted and spun.

***

Thanksgiving came and passed, I studied for finals, and the day arrived for our flight to France. During the intervening weeks since we'd stolen Helga's book, as we came to call it, there'd been no sign that she knew of the theft. Certainly, she hadn't sent anyone to Las Abs to come looking for her book. Word traveled fast if a new face showed up in our town, and we hadn't heard anything.

Still, Will and I breathed easier once we put Las Abuelitas and Merced behind us on our flight day. Our plane left from San Francisco, a non-stop to Paris/Charles de Gaulle airport. I had the window seat, Will sat in the middle, and Mickie had the aisle.

"In case I have to step into chaperone-mode early," she said.

Every now and again I heard Gwyn's low pitched belly-laugh above the hum of airplane passengers. I missed hanging out with her, missed her laughter. She'd avoided making eye contact during the entire three hours our group spent in SFO. With only twenty-four students, this trip would make it harder for us to ignore one another.

In any case, I felt blissfully happy to be sitting by Will for the eleven hour flight. Not that we could talk about any of the things we ached to discuss: what would Sir Walter be like, in the flesh? Would he be able to translate Pfeffer's black book? Had Pfeffer left him any messages to deliver in person? Would he be too old and decrepit to count on for any real help?

Will and I squandered the first hours playing cards with Mickie ("You cheated!" "Did not!") and drinking copious amounts of the free soft drinks offered every hour or two. Mick upgraded her beverage to wine as we crossed the Mississippi, and she drifted off to sleep a few hundred miles west of the Atlantic, lulled by the roar of the engines and the whine of a hundred headsets tuned to different movies.

Will didn't really fit in the tiny economy seat wedged between me and his sister. Every time his leg drifted over to Mickie's side, she'd awaken with a start, snarl at her brother, and shove his leg back. I tried to think of a non-awkward way to say to Will, R*est your legs against mine*.

Across the aisle, a young couple returning to France folded into one another so completely that I couldn't tell where one body began and the other ended. Comfort travel in the coach class. I glanced over at Will beside me, stiff and awkward, holding himself within the imaginary boundaries of his middle-seat.

I curled my knees up, collapsing them against the wall at my left. "Hey," I said to Will, pointing to the space in front of me. "Stretch out already. You look ridiculous all pretzeled in your seat."

"You sure?" he asked.

"Unless you got a way to fold your legs in thirds," I replied. "Besides, I like the fetal position." I hugged my arms around my knees.

Will grinned and thanked me, easing his long legs into the space where my feet had been a moment earlier.

"Oh, man," he said, "You have no idea how good that feels. It's like they built this plane for under-nourished pre-schoolers."

Mickie mumbled in her sleep and shot an elbow into Will's ribs.

"No respect for my personal space even when she's asleep," Will whispered, gently replacing her arm. "Sir Walter offered to upgrade our tickets to First Class, and Mick said no."

I raised my eyebrows.

"She takes stubborn to new heights," said Will.

"I thought you guys were passing him off as your rich French uncle."

"Maybe he's feeling the recession." Will yawned hugely. "I think I might be able to sleep now. How much longer?"

I consulted my cell. "Five and a half hours."

Will's eyes settled to half-mast. "Mmmm." He looked comfortable now that his legs had somewhere to rest. His eyes drifted shut.

My eyes followed the curve of space between us, a pathway of places where we didn't touch, where our bodies might intersect but didn't. Will's breathing settled until it matched his sister's.

My reading light cast an industrial white glow about me. Most other passengers had turned theirs off. I might have been the only person on the flight still awake. I should have drunk Sprite instead of Coke. Sighing, I pulled Helga's book from my bag and started flipping pages. Unfortunately, in the past three weeks, I'd begun to admit that we'd stolen something utterly useless. It was a book of names and dates and crisscross lines with no hint of a story or confession of evil schemes. I'd recognized no names so far except for "Napoleon" and a couple of "Helisaba's" like from Pfeffer's book, but nothing remotely useful had turned up. We'd undertaken that trip to UC Merced and exposed our underbellies with nothing to show for it.

Beside me Will twitched and mumbled something incomprehensible. His right side pushed up against his sister, but she was finally too crashed out to care. Another twitch and a small shift and now his cheek pressed into my shoulder, his legs articulating a curve around the front edge of my chair. I ached for how his hand would feel pressed into my hand. For his lips melting with mine. For wishing his head resting upon my shoulder meant something more than my-neck-got-tired.

I closed the book, nestling it into my bag. I closed my eyes upon the image of Will's form surrounding mine. Aching, wishing, breathing in the clean-washed scent of Will's hair, I wandered at last into sleep.

Excerpted from the private journal of Helga Gottlieb, circa present day

The time is ripe! The girl will be mine.

Hans has warned me that should some accident befall the girl, Father's retribution would be swift. I do not doubt that Father would kill me. As surely as he employed me to kill others of his children, he would employ one of them to dispatch me.

But only if he knew!

From this will come my triumph: I need not take the child from her sleepy home town. Oh, not at all! She travels to France! A mishap in France, while dutiful Helga works in her laboratory in California—such a thing could not be linked to me. I shall send Ivanovich for the girl. I trust no one else.

Oh, Father, I shall best you! Hans, you, too, shall bow before me in time. In the establishment of a New Race of Man, I shall be victorious.

To the victor go the spoils!

8

FRANCE

I woke to the sound of someone pounding on my door. *My dad,* I thought blearily as my eyes tried to make the darkened room resemble my bedroom.

Then I sat up, remembering I was in France—*in France!*

As I pulled socks and boots back on my feet, the door-pounding recommenced. I grabbed my bag and threw open the door.

"Never open a door if you don't know who is on the other side," barked Mickie, glaring at me. "Can you be ready in two minutes? We all overslept. Madame Evans is taking the group to the castle *now.*"

"Sure," I said, grabbing my jacket and bag.

I rubbed my eyes and recalled yesterday's travel. Or was it today's? The journey from San Francisco to

Paris had wearied us. The train to Tours and bus to Chenonceaux remained only a blur of jostlings and legs that fell asleep, hands that cramped clutching suitcase handles.

Sir Walter had suggested giving us twenty-four hours to acclimate before meeting him, and now I understood why. My eyes saw bright daylight, but my body protested it was only 3:00 in the morning in California.

Our connection with Sir Walter had proven a useful one for the French Club. Mickie's "rich uncle" would be our *host family*—well, host *person*—for a three-day home-stay where we would be sent off in pairs to experience the holidays with French families at the end of our two-week trip.

Sir Walter had also secured discounted group lodging for our first several days during a season when many hotels closed. Although apparently he didn't think much of elevators. Upon our arrival at the *Hôtel de Rose*, Chenonceaux, we hauled our bags up endless, narrow flights of stairs. I silently thanked Dad for making me pack light. Mick had her own room.

"The size of a half-bath," she whispered to Will and me as we sat in a group meeting designed to inform us that we were in France where the spoken language was French. We also received a lesson on currency and an envelope apiece with one lunch's-worth of Euros. Finally, we heard that we had the next two hours free until 1:00 PM when we would walk as a group to the Château de Chenonceau, the first of our Loire Valley castle-tours.

"I know what I'm doing with my two hours," said Will. "Sleeping."

"Wrong," said Mickie. "You're asking the French-speaking desk clerk if there are any messages from our uncle."

Will grunted in discontent, but shuffled from the small breakfast room into the lobby where he asked, in passable French, if there were any messages.

"*Non, monsieur,*" was an answer even Mickie could understand, and the three of us hiked up to our respective rooms.

That had been my first morning in France.

Now that it was afternoon, I finally felt awake. And hungry. My stomach demanded breakfast. Downstairs, Will had scored some croissants from a bakery next door to the hotel. Mickie berated him for wandering off, but she also took a croissant.

"You might have remembered coffee while you were at it," she grumbled.

"*She's allergic to morning,*" Will mouthed as he handed a pastry to me. We clomped along a quiet road behind Madame Evans, who seemed to have forgotten how to speak English since landing in France. Our group made enough noise to earn more than a few dour Gallic stares, human *and* canine, as we tromped past.

Upon arriving at Château de Chenonceau, our destination, we received entrance tickets and instructions to meet for the walk back to the hotel at 5:00 PM. Mickie took students to find restrooms; Will and I strolled together down an avenue of giant, leafless trees. A weak sun peered from behind thin clouds, and I wrapped my scarf once more around my neck as we crunched along the gravel drive. We moved past outbuildings and hibernating gardens, past stumps of knobby pruned trees, beside canals green with moss until at last, Chenonceau castle rose up before us.

"Hey look," Will said, raising a gloved hand and pointing. "Our first scaffolding." He snapped a picture. "For your step-mom."

Sylvia had told us the French took excellent care of their historical treasures, leaving the country in a state of constant repair. As we neared the *château*, I saw a formal garden to the right. Sylvia would love the winter blooms: red and white flowers amidst carefully trimmed hedges and geometric walkways. I didn't know what any of the flowering things were, only that they were unexpected in winter.

"Let's go up," I said. I pointed to leaded glass windows along the castle façade before us. "I want to take a picture of the garden from up there."

Will nodded.

"*Billets? Vos billets, s'il vous plaît,*" said a woman at the door. I couldn't have figured how to knot her elegant scarf if I'd had a year to attempt it.

"Tee-kets please, your tee-kets," she repeated in English. We held ours up for inspection and proceeded into the entrance hall. Nothing grand, hardly larger than the oversized entry to my own home thousands of miles away.

Will gestured to the stairs ahead and to the right. We marched up the cold white marble. This kind of floor would be heaven in Central California in the summer, but I didn't want to touch it in France in December.

"Imagine living here," Will said. "You'd need a ton of space heaters."

"Yeah."

At the top of the staircase, we turned left into a wide hallway, with doors leading off on either side. From one end of the hall, light danced through the windows, sparkling off the hundred tiny bits of leaded glass. My shoes squeaked on the highly polished floor.

"Wish we could open these for my picture." I brushed fingers along the window, smooth planes interrupted by ridges of ancient lead. "There's got to be windows open somewhere. Did you feel that draft?" I pulled out my camera.

From my second-story lookout, I discovered another, larger garden to the right, across a small waterway.

"I'm going in this room," Will said, leaving the hallway.

I could hear the rest of our group lumbering below, chattering loudly, announcing to one and all our identity as *les Americains*. I'd never felt uncomfortable with my nationality before. Okay, I'd never thought about it. But now, I couldn't help noticing how noisy Americans were compared to the French.

"Whoa," said Will, from the next room.

I crossed to join him.

"I just felt your breeze in here," Will said. "Where's it coming from?" He was walking from window to window, holding his hand out searching for the source of the cold air. "That was like—" he lowered his voice and I drew closer. "That was like touching *you* when you're invisible."

"Told you it was drafty," I said. "If I were rich enough to build a place like this, I'd insulate a lot better."

Will agreed and strolled into another room, connected to the first one.

"Hey, Sam, check this out."

I followed his voice.

"Oh!" I sighed.

The ante-room was tiny, perfect, paneled in ancient dark oak and covered with paintings of all sizes. But the real beauty was the open window and what you could see through it. Graceful arches stood sentry over water flowing lazily beneath the massive structure. All the pictures of the *château* showed this famous section of building.

"It's like a fairytale." My voice came out in a sigh.

Will watched me nervously as I gazed at the water. "Careful, Sam. Don't go blissing out."

I steadied my gaze on the grey-green flow of river. Hidden from his eyes, my mouth formed a smirk, and I decided to tease Will. I watched the water, then felt my flesh dissolve.

"Sam!" Will moaned. "You disappeared. Quick, come back. No more looking at the river. Our group could be here any minute."

He twisted to look over his shoulder for oncoming hordes. But I had listened carefully before vanishing, and I knew no one was coming yet. I walked towards Will and gave him an enormous icy embrace. Then, because I found the temptation irresistible, I brushed my lips along the back of his neck. Ignoring the winged creatures flapping in my stomach, I turned towards the ancient wall. At this point I felt a tickle of curiosity. What would it feel like, smell like, to pass through a wall this ancient and into the corridor?

Will called my name again. I made sure no one else was approaching and entered the wall. The wall measured perhaps eighteen inches thick. Inside I sensed cold stone and furniture polish and wood that had once been tree. Behind me, Will groaned, so I shivered back through the wall oh-so-slowly and then rippled solid.

Will sighed in relief.

I grinned and didn't say anything.

He frowned. "Tell me you didn't do that on purpose."

I grinned bigger.

"That was irresponsible," he said, glaring.

"This, from the guy who likes to break into evil laboratories for fun?" I asked.

"Hmmph," he grunted. "Let's go check out the other rooms." We returned to the central hall.

I picked a room on the opposite side and Will followed me.

"Brr! How could anyone stay warm enough to sleep here?" I asked, walking towards an ancient carved bed.

I snapped a quick picture of Will framed by the doorway, freezing in pixels a furrow deepening along his forehead.

"What's with the frown?" I asked. "You mad at me? Will, I checked to make sure no one was around. I'm not stupid."

"No, no—not that."

We heard our fellow-students thumping up the marble staircase.

"Later," he said.

Madame Evans arrived in the hall, describing a love affair between a French king and the woman to whom he had presented this *château*.

"Nice gift," Will said, as he gravitated towards the sound of a history lesson he might miss. In Las Abs, I smiled indulgently at his obsession. Here in France, history crooked her finger at Will around every corner.

As Madame left, Will whispered into my ear. "A minute ago, I felt that chill you were talking about. Do you think the cold spots are, well, moving around a lot?"

I shivered from the warmth of his breath on my neck and ear—so close, so intimate.

"You mean, someone like us? Here?" I asked.

Will nodded, curt. He mouthed two words: *a rippler.*

I shook my head. "We're getting as paranoid as your sister."

I circled the room once more, my fingers trailing wide to detect any change of temperature, but I felt nothing. Madame Evans led us through two additional rooms on the second floor before herding us up one level. I heard Gwyn's laughter echoing through the high-ceilinged stairwell. I tried not to miss her friendship.

"Maybe it's ghosts," whispered Will. "*Madame, s'il vous plaît?*" He was addressing our French teacher.

She turned. "*Oui?*"

"*Sont-ils des histoires des fantômes du château?*"

"*Mais non*," she replied. "*Ce château, c'est un château des dames, et de l'amour, pas des fantômes.*"

"A 'castle of women and of love,'" I said to Will.

He looked disappointed. "Guess we have to rule out ghosts."

We continued with Madame and our classmates until we'd seen the entire castle. Mickie joined us as we explored the kitchens below ground.

"Where've you been, Mick?" Will asked.

"The kitchen gardens," she said enthusiastically. "Back by the entrance to the grounds. I had a very cool composting lesson. Using hand gestures. God, I wish I'd taken French. That was some gorgeous dirt."

Will and I gagged back laughter, Will turning his into a evil-sounding cough.

"We're heading to the formal garden with the fountain in the middle," I said. "I think that's where they take the pictures looking back upriver at the castle."

Mickie joined us and we set off across a graveled walk. The ground stone dusted my black boots in pale powder. We had just descended a set of stairs into the garden when I heard Will's sudden intake of breath.

"What?" I asked.

"Did you feel that?"

"What?" I asked.

"That wash of cold," he whispered.

"No," Mickie and I said together.

"I'd swear someone *like us* just passed through me. Like an icy blast"

"A friendly blast? Or, you know . . ." I broke off.

Will rolled his eyes at me. "*Friendly*? How am I supposed to tell?"

"Keep your voice down," said Mickie. "How sure are you, Will?"

"What I felt was just like when Sam walked through me a minute ago," he replied.

Not hard to guess how Mickie was going to view my behavior.

She groaned, cursed, and pressed her thumb and forefinger to her eyes. "Please tell me you were alone."

"Of course," I said, flushing.

"Oh, great, now someone's staring at us," Mickie said, eyeing a gentleman who *did* seem to be looking at us with curiosity. "Get your picture and we're moving on," she whispered.

I took some quick snapshots, matching the view of the castle I'd seen on guidebooks and postcards.

Will and his sister marched back to the stairs. I followed, but twisted to capture one last shot of the formal garden. I nearly bumped into staring-man, walking just behind me.

"*Je suis désolé, Mademoiselle*," he apologized.

"*De rien.*" I told him it was nothing and dashed to Mickie and Will. My heart pounded and I tried to convince myself it was a coincidence that someone would choose to stare at us. We were six-thousand miles from UC Merced and this guy looked genteel French, not *übermensch*-y.

Leaving the staring man behind, we retraced our way to the entrance, beside the knobby-bald trees and winter-dead vegetable gardens. As we approached the grand avenue, a path joined ours from the side, and the same gentleman strolled towards us, gazing at us as if to memorize each of our faces. Or discover our weaknesses.

This time, Will stepped out to confront him, placing himself between us and the stranger. "*Que voulez-vous, Monsieur?*"

"Will asked him what he wants," I whispered to Mickie.

The grey-haired man smiled and replied in crisp English. "A great many things, young man, none of which pose any threat to you or your . . . companions." He inclined his head to Mickie and myself, a polite, antiquated gesture.

Mickie bristled. "Our conversation is private, if you don't mind."

"Certainly," he said, a hint of a smile pulling at one side of his mouth. "I beg your pardon." He looked intently in several directions and then nodding once again, he began walking down the avenue of silent trees and disappeared into thin air.

"Holy shit!" Mickie whispered.

9

SIR WALTER DE ROCHEFORT

"Monsieur de Rochefort?" Will called softly after him.

"No, Will!" Mickie looked in exasperation at her brother. "We don't know who that was."

"He looked *friendly*, alright? Who else could he be?" asked Will.

As if in response, a spot before one of the great mottled trunks shimmered and resolved itself into the old man.

"*Bonjour, Mesdemoiselles, Monsieur.* Allow me to present myself. I am called Waldhart Jean-Baptiste de Rochefort, and I am entirely at your service." He made a seriously old-fashioned bow before crunching along the drive toward us.

"You speak English really good," Will said.

"I speak English very *well*," corrected the grey-haired gentleman. He then pulled himself up to his full height somewhere just below my own five-foot-seven and drew in a breath through his nose, so exaggeratedly that his nostrils almost pinched shut. "We French invented English, as a means of communicating to the miserable peasants inhabiting that forsaken island known as Greater Bretagne."

His hauteur suggested we might belong to the miserable peasant contingency.

"Ten-sixty-six," said Will.

The old gentleman tilted his head to one side and down, an understated nod.

I looked at Will, lost.

"The French conquered England in 1066," Will murmured in explanation. "The English language came into being as the conquerors and the defeated figured out how to talk to each other."

The Frenchman regarded Will with something like approval. "You evidently share the Conqueror's name, Guillaume."

"No, I was named after a river in Oregon," Will said.

"You know my brother's name?" Mickie asked. "Pfeffer kept that secret."

"There's a Guillaume River in Oregon?" I asked.

"Willamette River," Will replied.

"So that's your real name, *Willamette*?" I asked.

"My real name is Will," he replied tersely.

"How do you know my brother's name?" Mickie repeated, an edge to her voice.

The ghostly Frenchman, ignoring Mickie's question, continued dismissively, "Of course, you are Americans, with your own bastardization of the island dialect."

"I flew six thousand miles to meet you and *now* you're telling me you have a problem with Americans?" Mickie asked, eyes narrowing.

"Of course not. The French *love* Americans. We gave your country to you two times over as a gesture of our goodwill. First was the Marquis de Lafayette, and later our own Napoleon sold half your nation to you for pennies. Without France there would be no America."

"Napoleon wasn't French," Will muttered.

The old man regarded Will. "Napoleon was *la France*," he said, as if he'd thrown down a glove and now waited for Will to retrieve it. The exchange left me puzzled, but Will nodded as if conceding the point.

"But we gave you Paris in 1944, so we're even," said Will.

"*Touché*," whispered the gentleman, a hint of a smile as he gazed at Will.

The old man fixed Mickie with an imperious gaze. "As for my knowing the name of your brother, *chère*

Mademoiselle Mackenzie, I took care that I should know both his name and his identity before revealing myself."

Here he turned from Mickie to gaze upon me.

"*Bonjour Mademoiselle,*" he said.

"*Bonjour,* Sir Walter," I said politely. Then I blushed and stammered. "I mean *Monsieur de Rocheforte.*"

"*Non, non,*" he said. "You have not misspoken. But how did you know of my knighthood?"

"Knighthood?" asked Mickie.

"We didn't know at all," said Will. "I, uh, started referring to you as 'Sir Walter' back home. I got everyone else in the habit. Sorry."

"As a speaker of English, it is most fit you would adjust my name from Waldhart to Walter." A smile twitched along his mouth. "And you are welcome to continue to address me by my title as Sir Walter." The small smile grew to a larger one.

He turned back to study me. "This is a cousin perhaps?" he asked Will and Mickie. "Not, I think, your sister."

"Samantha is our friend," Will said. Lowering his voice he whispered, "She's the one we wrote you about."

Sir Walter's mouth curved upwards. "*Mademoiselle Samanthe, Waldhart Jean-Baptiste de Rochefort, à vôtre service.*"

My face heated, from trying not to laugh at his old-fashioned manners.

"Okay, listen. So, how do we know you are who you say you are?" Mickie asked.

Sir Walter shrugged—a gesture the French should totally trademark—and answered. "You cannot, of course. You can only accept that before you is the man with whom you have corresponded, or you can choose not to accept. Allow me, however, to point out that if I wished to do you harm, that could have been accomplished several hours ago. I also know which one of you I would keep hold of as a hostage should I wish to force your brother and friend to remain in solid form."

"You watched us upstairs, inside the castle, when we were alone," I said.

He looked puzzled. "I did, indeed, watch you and your friends, *Mademoiselle*, but only whilst you were out of doors."

"You placed yourself in my path while you were invisible," said Will.

"Your reactions helped me to be sure of your identities," Sir Walter said. "I never form an acquaintance without reassuring myself that there has been no trap lain for me by a clever enemy."

"Dude." Will smiled. "You're going to get along great with my sister."

Mickie frowned, uncertain whether to trust him.

"But *Mademoiselle Samanthe*, what is this you say of being watched indoors?"

"We noticed—Will and I noticed—an icy presence in the castle."

Sir Walter's brows drew together ever so slightly. "I should have made a more thorough search." His heavy lids closed and he seemed to disappear inside himself. Then he opened his eyes again. "You appear to have captured the interest of a person with whom I am well acquainted. Him, I have found relatively harmless, all things considered. He fears me greatly." The French gentleman smiled and drew himself tall. "You are to consider yourselves under my protection. Whether you can see me or not, I shall guard your well-being."

"That's very kind of you to offer to protect us," said Mickie. You could see it on her face: she was stuck halfway between impressed that the French gentleman had bad-guy radar and worried he wouldn't be able to offer much assistance.

"Not at all," said Sir Walter, bowing. "Pfeffer would have expected it."

"How do you 'see' an invisible person's identity?" asked Will.

The Frenchman shrugged. "Assuming I have already encountered the person, it is simple enough for me to recognize the signature of their thoughts, while they are invisible."

"Simple for you," murmured Will, his admiration evident.

"Okay," said Mickie. "So that brings me to my next problem. Assuming you're Sir Walter, I need to know why we should trust you. For starters, why did Professor Pfeffer trust you?"

Sir Walter made a small sort of laugh. "You might turn that question on its head and ask why I trusted him. However, to answer your question, he trusted me from the moment I saved his life." He smiled as if he would say no more on that subject. "I believe there is an hour before you depart with your group?"

We nodded.

"It would be well if we conversed in privacy, yes?" Gesturing with a sweep of his hand, Sir Walter led us off the main roadway, to the side path we'd seen him upon minutes ago.

We arrived at a small arrangement of iron chairs and a table and sat.

"On the occasion of our last visit together, Doctor Pfeffer confided to me his discovery of yourself and your brother. He spoke of you in terms of highest praise." His smile turned downwards as if he were now remembering something unpleasant. "We agreed that should he find himself in danger, he would leave important documents in your keeping and that I should contact you in this event. He spoke of his plan to obtain a record of Helmann's experiments upon children during the Second World War. I attempted to dissuade him, to point out the danger of drawing attention to himself by such a theft, but he would not listen."

"He was stubborn," said Mickie.

"Look who's talking," mumbled Will.

"A strong will is a great asset," said Sir Walter, his mouth pulling into half a smile. "Especially for one without other genetic gifts. *Mademoiselle*, I understand you do not share your brother's abilities?"

Mickie shook her head. "I can't ripple."

"You are not a 'chameleon'?" Sir Walter asked. "That is the word I use. Quite aside from the chameleon's ability to disappear, the creature was for centuries thought to live by consuming only air." He laughed softly to himself. "What is your word again? Ree-pill?"

"Ripple. It's like when you disturb a pool of water, you know, the ripples that flow out. That's what it looks like when Will disappears," Mickie replied.

"Of course. A good word. Especially as there is no verb-form of 'chameleon.' Trust my young friend Pfeffer to find a better word in the language of his new home," said Sir Walter.

"It's *my* word," snapped Mickie. "Pfeffer referred to Will's ability as 'the phenomenon' before I told him my word."

Will snickered at his sister's prickliness.

Sir Walter spoke gently. "He would have been only too quick to credit you, my dear, were he here with us now."

Mickie's eyes dropped. The kind words about her former advisor appeased her. "Okay, listen," she said. "I believe you're Sir Walter. I believe Pfeffer trusted you. But for the love of all that's holy, why didn't you stick to our plan to meet up in Amboise?"

"Ah, yes." Sir Walter looked self-consciously at the table-top before us. "I have waited so long. You must forgive me for meeting you thus unannounced. I found I preferred to wait no longer. You must forgive an impatient old man; the old are of course incorrigible." He smiled at us and then turned his gaze towards the sky, now clear of clouds.

Mickie stared at him for a moment and then smiled. "Yeah, okay, we forgive you."

Sir Walter returned his gaze from the heavens. His lips tightened and thinned as he addressed us. "I am in hopes that you have brought the manuscript for which I believe my dear friend was killed."

The black book. Now came the moment of truth. Did Mickie trust Sir Walter enough to hand over the writings?

She stared hard at the old gentleman, then slowly nodding her head, she withdrew the book from her bag and surrendered it to him.

"We had trouble reading it," she said.

Sir Walter's lip curled into a smile. "I should imagine. It is the language of my youth, spoken in Helmann's childhood, but no longer common."

Suddenly I was the one with trust issues. "You're not . . . you aren't the man who wrote it, are you?" The words tumbled out, echoing like an accusation.

Sir Walter looked up from the black book at my question. "No, child. I am not Helmann. But he and I have a shared history; he is my cousin, whom I once knew as *Girard L'Inferne*."

The cold iron of the chair made its way through my jeans, and I shivered, pulling my scarf higher.

Sir Walter spoke. "For a very long time, Pfeffer urged me to act upon knowledge I held regarding my cousin, the man credited with discovering the chameleon disease. To my shame I did nothing. Or very little. At great personal risk, Pfeffer obtained this record of offenses with which he hoped to damn my cousin."

"I'm sorry to doubt you, but no way did Pfeffer risk death just to show the world how some dead Nazi-dude used to be evil," said Will.

"Dead?" Sir Walter looked at us, gaze intense. "No, unfortunately Helmann is very much alive. And more dangerous than ever." Sir Walter took out a small French cigarette. "Do you mind?"

None of us had the nerve to tell him he couldn't smoke.

"How old would you say I am?" he asked.

"We were expecting someone in their upper-eighties," said Mickie. "But you look maybe fifty."

"You're older than that, aren't you?" I asked.

"You three have discovered one of the advantages of being a chameleon?" replied Sir Walter. "I'm surprised Pfeffer taught you of this."

"He didn't," said Will. "Sam thought of it."

I'd suggested that maybe Will looked younger than his eighteen years because he'd spent so much time invisible when he was little.

"You will not age during the minutes or hours when you *ree-pill*, as you call it," said Sir Walter.

Mickie's face had gone pale. "So Helmann is a *chameleon* as well?"

Sir Walter nodded. "Very well deduced, *Mademoiselle*."

"Helmann, the same Helmann, now controls Geneses," Mickie said, looking anxious. "Of course. *Of course*. He alone was able to distinguish between Helmann's disease and leprosy in an age where genes couldn't be examined. He understood the difference because he was a carrier himself."

"Precisely," said Sir Walter.

"So, if you don't mind my asking," said Mickie, "how old exactly are you and Dr. Helmann?"

"We were born to sisters-in-law in the same year, being the tenth after the onset of the Papal Schism," he replied.

"No way." Will laughed at the old man.

I didn't get the joke.

"As in, *the* Papal Schism?" asked Mickie, looking doubtful.

Will turned to me. "The Papal Schism occurred when two separate Popes were elected following the removal of the Papal court from Avignon, France back to Rome. Only that's impossible." He squinted, looking at Sir Walter. "That would make you . . ." He broke off, trying to calculate.

"I am a quarter-century past my six-hundredth birthday," Sir Walter announced, wreathing all of us in the smoke of his *gauloises* cigarette.

Excerpted from My Father's Brilliant Journey, by Helga Gottlieb

Early Years

In speaking of my father's development as the Savior of Mankind, it is impossible to underestimate the importance of his early years; that is, the years prior to age sixteen, when he began to live regularly as a chameleon.

My father was the only child of a nobleman's second son born at the close of the 14th century, CE.* Underprivileged, as such families of younger sons often were, my father also lost his parents during the conflicts with Northern Frenchmen and was raised through the so-called charity of his aunt, the Lady de Rochefort, wealthy and of noble birth. Her own daughter, Helisaba (or Elisabeth) de Rochefort, eventually became wife to my father.

But for years prior to my father's accession to a noble inheritance, he had to endure the petty injuries and daily insults accompanying the lives of those born in unfortunate circumstances. His cousin Waldhart (later known as Walter de Rochefort) in particular delighted in inventing new torments for the young Girard.

Chief of these was the unfortunate appending to my father's name of "L'Inferne." The nickname, alternately translatable as "fire," "fiery one," "Hell," or even, "Hell-ish one," ultimately became adopted by my father as part of the name by which we know him today. So, while the miscreant Waldhart intended the name as a form of abuse, ultimately my father transcended his cousin's intentions and adopted the name by which we have all been saved, Girard Helmann.

*In fairness to my father's system of beliefs, I could use A.D., but as I myself am not a believer in such antiquated constructs, I choose to use the designation "Christian Era" instead of Anno Domini, or "Year of our Lord." It is my hope to bring about a system of B.H.E. or Before Helmannic Era and P.H.E. or Post Helmannic Era in the future.

10

"The destruction of the Mayan Empire," said Will, the following morning. "And Timbuktu, the Battle of Agincourt, the Turkish capture of Constantinople, the Spanish Armada . . ." Will continued chanting his strange rosary as we made the short hike from the Castle of Amboise to the smaller Clos-Lucé, final home of Leonardo da Vinci. We'd all slept remarkably well, considering that we'd met a six-hundred-year-old man the previous day.

"What's he muttering about?" I asked Mickie.

She shrugged. "Who knows? Used to fall asleep with a copy of Encyclopedia Britannica on his face."

"Does he do this reciting thing often, then?"

Will broke off at "Hideyoshi attacks Korea," and turned to Mickie and me. "Don't you see? These are all events Sir Walter *lived* through—things he heard about first-hand. It's *amazing!*" His arms flew wide like he was conducting a symphony.

"I'm more interested in what he's seen in the last seventy years, myself," said Mickie. "Or the last *decade,* since the human genome was mapped."

"Yeah," I said. "No kidding."

"When's he meeting us today?" Will asked.

"Given his flair for drama?" Mickie shrugged. "Expect him when we see him."

Or when we don't *see him,* I thought. Aloud I observed, "He's certainly different from what I expected."

"Yeah, lots of swagger for such a short little dude." said Will.

"People used to be smaller," said Mickie. "I bet Da Vinci's bed is short."

"Sir Walter could have *met* Da Vinci, you know?" Will's eyes took on a faraway, transfixed quality as we approached Leonardo's last home.

"Will's biggest hero," Mickie explained.

We took the tour with our group through Da Vinci's modest *château* and then found ourselves released with two hours before the bus took us back to the hotel. Most of our group headed for the gift shop and *chocolat-chaud* at the snack bar, but Will wanted to view an exhibit of Leonardo's inventions more than any of us wanted to drink hot chocolate.

"He had ideas for flying machines, tanks, and all kinds of stuff that no one else tried to make for centuries." Will's enthusiasm proved contagious, and we followed him only to find Sir Walter waiting for us in contemplation of a drawing that did, indeed, resemble a tank from modern warfare.

"Ah, *bonjour*, my friends," said the French gentleman. "You are enjoying Amboise today?"

"Totally!" said Will.

"Clos-Lucé is a special place. I often spend time here during the slow season. Fewer tourists." He smiled at us.

"Did you know him? Leonardo?" Will kept his voice low and directed towards our quartet only.

"We met. My cousin befriended him first, however. I can still recall my cousin's interest in these machines of war." Sir Walter paused to gesture to a drawing of a gun that could fire multiple times before requiring re-loading. "It took centuries for Girard to find generals and engineers who exploited these possibilities." The old man sighed heavily. "I should have stopped him then, or at least tried . . ."

Will spoke softly. "Your cousin was French like you, right?"

"We wondered because the stories seem to be set in Nazi Germany," I added.

"Girard saw more promise in the German State for his own ambitions of domination. He had long since abandoned any loyalty to *la France*." Sir Walter looked around. "Shall we remove to where there are fewer ears, yes?" He began walking, beckoning us to follow.

We trekked into the wintry grounds below the *château*, the only ones choosing this route back to the bus.

"The book you so kindly placed in my possession is no work of fiction; it is a journal recording the day-to-day thoughts and discoveries of my cousin Helmann. He has been a keeper of diaries all his life. This *particular* black book is but one of hundreds."

Will shot me a look that said, *We were right!*

Sir Walter continued. "He believes that when, one day, he dominates all of the world, these journals will be invaluable to his biographers."

Will mimed making himself puke.

"Professor Pfeffer may have given the book to you, my dear," here he looked at Mickie, "but he always intended it to raise *me* from inaction."

"I don't understand," said Mickie.

As we waited for his response, the old man pressed fingers to the corners of his eyes. Tears?

"I have been a selfish creature. As bad, in my own way, as my cousin. Helmann *acted* according to principles, however diseased. I have rarely been led to action by my own principles. Pfeffer believed that I needed a reminder as to why I should act against my cousin. The experiments recorded in that journal are intended to, how do you say . . . light a blaze beneath my *derrière*."

"So, if the man keeping the journal was Helmann," began Will, "What was up with all the kid-torture? Sam thinks he was trying to create some kind of Special Forces."

"An astute guess." Sir Walter nodded at me. "Conditions in Germany during the Second World War allowed Helmann the opportunity to raise from infancy an especially loyal group of followers, some of whom serve him to this day.

"At the war's end, I rescued Pfeffer from Helmann's abandoned compound. Pfeffer was a child of ten years. Girard had already taken four of his favorite children to South America once it became clear Germany would lose the war. Of those who remained imprisoned, only Pfeffer and two girls were still in health when I arrived. I placed the girls, who were not chameleons, with kind German families. Pfeffer, I raised myself. It was clear to me even then that he had chosen a different path from my cousin."

"So Pfeffer *did* grow up with those kids," Will said. "Like Sam thought."

"Unbelievable," said Mickie. "But, wait—Pfeffer wasn't a chameleon. He would have told me."

Sir Walter looked thoughtful. "He must have decided it was not in the best interest of your safety to know that of him. Yes, he was a chameleon. But he did not choose to live as one. This was one of our great disagreements. Some thirty years ago, Pfeffer began to take the Neuroprine drug to counteract his abilities."

I raised my eyebrows in surprise.

Sir Walter continued. "However, he monitored the drug's effects upon mice so that he would know if one day Girard decided to destroy the gene pool of potential chameleons through the use of a tainted drug."

"Why wouldn't Pfeffer want to maintain his ability to ripple?" I asked.

"We argued constantly over his choice to deny his true nature as a chameleon. He told me there was no choice—that for him, the ability was tied to Girard, that is, *Helmann,* and his aims. He chose to live an ordinary lifespan as a *distillation* of his rejection of his father."

"You just said his *father.*" Mickie's face turned ashen.

"Ah, yes. But more of that later." Sir Walter gestured to the clusters of students arriving at the bus.

Mick wasn't about to quit asking questions. Lowering her voice, she herded us away from the bus. "Okay, listen, Sir Walter. The history lesson was nice and all, but what we're really here for is to fight

Helmann, right? And I for one would like to start as soon as humanly possible."

Sir Walter regarded her with amusement. "Indeed, I thought you were here," he gestured towards the students, "to learn about *La Belle France.* Unless your school system provides such opportunities on a regular basis?"

Mickie fumed. "Oh, come on. You know what I mean. *I'm* not here to learn about France."

"How charmingly *Américaine,*" said Sir Walter, looking anything but charmed.

Mick scowled.

"I shall have completed my translation of the black book by morning," said the French gentleman in cool tones. "I will provide copies for each of you to examine as you travel tomorrow."

"My sister meant no disrespect, Sir Walter," said Will, glancing at his sister like she might contradict him. "It's just that we've come a long ways to meet you, and we were hoping, especially after that video you sent, to do something a little more . . . you know, badass."

Sir Walter chuckled and patted Will's shoulder. "My dear young man. Rest assured the time will come for that. In the meanwhile, are you perhaps familiar with the phrase about the doom awaiting those who do not appreciate *L'Histoire?*"

Will rattled off the familiar quote. "Those who don't study history are doomed to repeat it. Jorge Santayana."

"An adequate, if imperfect, rendering of what *Monsieur* Santayana wrote," said Sir Walter. "My dear children," (here Mickie bristled like a pinecone,) "Allow me to reassure you that if haste were necessary, we should act swiftly. You must understand that neither Girard nor I regard time in an altogether *normal* fashion. A year, or even ten years, we regard as a tiny nothing."

"Meanwhile the clock's ticking for the rest of us," muttered Mickie.

Sir Walter smiled. "Indeed. Your friends await you even now," he said, gesturing to the bus.

We climbed aboard, Mick grabbing two seats to herself, Will and I sitting together.

Across the aisle and up a few seats, I noticed Gwyn nodding her head as another student whispered and pointed at me. When the whisperer noticed that I observed her, she stopped mid-sentence and turned her face forward. No longer staring at me, she continued to drop quiet somethings about me into Gwyn's listening ear. A quiver ran through me—an involuntary shudder as I remembered the silent years when I'd decided I wouldn't talk to anyone. When they'd made fun of me. But Gwyn didn't giggle. And she didn't make faces at me. No, what she did wounded me far more deeply. She ignored me.

I forced myself to pay attention to Will, still flushed with the thrill of having walked where Leonardo Da Vinci once walked. Finally, Will appeared to have talked himself out on the subject and we switched to a discussion of Sir Walter. The chatter of twenty-four students created sufficient white noise, especially when half of them were ear-budded to electronic devices. Among other things, we wondered if we should give the book we'd stolen from Helga to Sir Walter.

"We need to wait for a chance to tell him when my sister's not in the room," said Will.

"Right," I agreed. "And I guess he's got his hands full with translating Pfeffer's volume for now. Although, no matter what's inside it, I don't think the journal Pfeffer stole is going to be enough to make people turn against Dr. Helmann," I said. "I mean, the kind of people who would sit through the video presentation we watched without denouncing him for it, I don't think they're going to be all that disturbed by what he did to a handful of children in the last century."

Will nodded. "But Sir Walter's not stupid; I don't think those guys at the presentation are the ones he's planning to persuade."

"Do you think he's going to the government?"

"I don't know. Maybe." Will looked behind us at his sister, who was sleeping with ear-plugs. "I looked at the Geneses website back on the hotel computer. Helmann's name isn't anywhere to be seen."

"He ought to be *dead* by now. Plus, it wouldn't make sense for him to be listed under the name he used during World War Two, would it? The name of a war criminal?"

"Guess not. I found one name I recognized on the Geneses site, though. Our friend *Hans* is listed there."

I shuddered involuntarily at the mention of my mother's murderer.

"You okay?" asked Will.

"Um, yeah, I'm just . . . it's all so . . ."

"I know," said Will, smiling and taking my hand in his.

I looked down at the way our hands fit together. Perfectly.

Excerpted from My Father's Brilliant Journey, by Helga Gottlieb

Reflecting back upon an important lesson learned during the siege of Château Rochefort, my father writes:

Du Lac's soldiers held Waldhart, myself, and Lady de Rochefort, whom they seemed afeared to harm. This fear they overcame when Du Lac himself arrived. Du Lac threatened Waldhart and myself before my Lady; she flinched not, neither did she reveal aught when they began to prick and draw forth her blood.

Helisaba, my little cousin, however, could not watch this unmoved. She came solid from her chameleon-safety. Our enemies did not notice. They merely saw a child appearing seemingly from nowhere, as children do.

Du Lac placed the blade at tiny Helisaba's neck; still Lady de Rochefort revealed not whether her husband's men would come by valley or by mountain. I did not, at that time, believe any of us in mortal danger.

In short, I misjudged.

Du Lac changed tactics and released Lisaba, placing the blade at my Lady de Rochefort's own white neck. My cousin shrieked and could only be calmed by Du Lac insisting he had no wish to kill her lady-mother. Lisaba quieted and Du Lac asked her, upon pain of executing her mother, from whence would her father's soldiers issue?

Helisaba held her tongue as we all had been taught. Du Lac rose, sighed as one who rises from a good dinner, and swiftly spilled Lady de Rochefort's lifeblood. Lisaba whitened as though her own lifeblood ebbed with that of her mother. I ran, desperate to shield my little cousin, who fainted into my arms. For my weakness, we paid dearly.

Du Lac, sensing my affection for Helisaba, put the knife to her throat and asked me the question.

"Swear first that you will not harm her," I demanded.

Behind the soldiers, Waldhart cursed my name, calling all manner of dire blights upon me should I reveal what I knew and upon Du Lac should he harm Lisaba. The soldiers clapped his mouth shut.

"You have my word," said Du Lac.

I hesitated, uncertain as to the value of the word of a traitor. "Call down Heaven's curse should you break your word."

Du Lac laughed softly, straightened, and crossed himself. "May God damn my soul to the everlasting flames of Hell should I break my word and harm this child." He crossed himself again. "But I swear she dies if you do not speak, boy."

Helisaba, recovered from her faint, shook her head: No, Girard.

"They come by way of the mountain," said I.

Du Lac released Lisaba and lifting me by my shoulders, he stared into my eyes. "Swear it by the same oath I invoked."

This I could not do, for fear of my soul's well-being. I spoke the truth. "By the valley, then, may God bar me from Heaven should I lie."

By the frailty of my human heart, I had saved Lisaba. The battle, we lost.

I vowed never again to allow weakness to rule the day.

11

PARIS

We departed the Loire Valley the following morning with translations of Helmann's Nazi-era journals in hand. Sir Walter did not travel with us, promising instead to meet us in Paris. As I read the translated journal, I couldn't decide which disturbed me more: the experiments Helmann had designed or his musings upon the results. I put the translation down after one quick read-through, but Mickie pored through it again and again, making notes in the margins. What would Sir Walter make of the journal we had stolen from Helga? I itched to know if we had wasted our efforts, but I had no desire to break my word to Will. So far Mickie had always accompanied us when Sir Walter showed up.

We arrived at our Paris hotel in time for an 8:30PM dinner at an *Auvergnois* restaurant where every last student opted for cheesy potatoes, passing on the dish involving intestines. Tomorrow would be our first of four full days in Paris, and Sir Walter said he'd join us, invisibly or solid, for most of our group field trips. Our fourth day, the French Club trip *free day*, he instructed us to reserve for a special day-long outing; his eyes twinkled but he refused to reveal our destination.

At the Hotel Georges IV, I received a closet-sized single room, which suited me fine, but Mickie's room had been upgraded to a two-room suite.

"Gorgeous!" was how Mickie described the rooms she shared with her brother. "And yours is certainly . . . cozy," she said upon greeting me at my door the next morning. "You should come stay with us. Save you from a few bruises. Will can sleep on the couch in the sitting room."

"I'm sure he'll thank you for that."

She pushed the elevator call button. "He suggested it, so we can stay up together for late-nights with Sir Walter. And now that I've seen your doll-sized accommodations . . ." She shook her head. "What part of 'elbow room' do the French not get?"

After a hurried breakfast of crusty baguettes and strawberry jam, we stepped outside with our group. Sir Walter stood conversing in French with Madame

Evans. A bright sun greeted us as we departed our Latin-Quarter lodgings and trekked to Notre Dame Cathedral. Following a ten minute introduction to the history of the cathedral, Madame Evans released us to explore on our own for an hour.

The sheer, monstrous size of the building overwhelmed us.

"How'd they do this without cranes?" Will asked.

"Impressive, is it not?" replied Sir Walter. "I always enjoy being in the presence of an older *woman*." He chuckled to himself.

Mickie looked at him blankly and Will interpreted. "Notre Dame means 'Our Lady,' Mick. And she's a couple hundred years older than present company."

Present Company directed us to a quiet apse. "Did you find your reading enlightening?"

I nodded my head *yes*.

Mickie's "Fascinating!" overlapped with Will's "Creepy."

Sir Walter continued. "The stories are familiar to me, from conversations with Pfeffer, but they make for disturbing reading, nonetheless."

"Speaking of disturbing," Mickie said, "You sent an article on Neuroprine deaths in France. We've seen something similar in the U.S."

Sir Walter listened.

"So, do you have a plan to halt these occurrences?" asked Mickie. "'Cause that's pretty much number one on my *to do* list."

"We fight a desperate battle," Sir Walter replied. "Allow me to share some of our opponent's past accomplishments."

"Here we go with the history," muttered Mickie.

"You recall the map I sent to you?" asked the French gentleman.

"Sure," said Will.

Sir Walter asked, "Are you able to recall to mind the lands which were lacking in markings of red?"

Mickie and Will nodded. I couldn't remember the map like they did.

"The markings indicate concentrations of known Helmann's carriers. The areas lacking red are areas where Helmann was free to *eliminate* known carriers during the Nazi reign."

"A genetic purge," Mickie whispered.

Sir Walter spoke. "Yes."

"Pfeffer kept us in the dark about *so much,*" Mickie said.

"No doubt he intended to keep you safer, knowing less," said Sir Walter. "As you can guess, he and I disagreed upon that." The old man sighed softly.

I used the pause to whisper a question. "Why did Helmann want a purge? Either time?" It was the question of a child who still needed to understand her mother's death.

"Why, indeed? Can you think of no reason to eliminate such a trait from a population?" Sir Walter's eyes drifted to the clerestory windows.

"There's an obvious benefit if you *controlled* those who carry the trait," said Will. "And if you eliminate those you can't control, you could have a monopoly on invisibility. Or raise an invisible army."

"Your supposition is correct. This goal drives my cousin. It has driven him for . . . let us say, a long while."

Will shifted on his feet, leaning in and lowering his voice. "So he plans to control anyone who has this ability . . ."

Sir Walter nodded. "And to reproduce additional *controlled* chameleons by all means available, genetic or conventional."

Will spoke softly. "So, we know who's behind the headlines we've been following, and we have a good idea of what he hopes to achieve. Is it time to call in Scotland Yard or the French FBI or something? You need us to testify?"

I nodded. "If we go to the media and explain how he operates by *showing what we can do*, the CIA or whoever would know what they're up against. We take away his secret advantage."

Sir Walter raised one tremendous eyebrow, glared at me. "No indeed, child. Think it through. Expose yourselves and how long do you think your family members have to live?"

I flushed, my heart skipping beats as I contemplated the fury I'd been ready to unleash upon Dad and Sylvia.

Sir Walter, pulling at the goatee upon his chin, sighed and continued. "You've both done well to conceal your true natures and keep yourselves hidden from Helmann. If he knew of you, you would be forced to follow him, or refusing that, he would consume you like the bloated spider he is. He has no tolerance for others like himself over whom he can exert no control."

"He killed Pfeffer," Mickie whispered. "Because he couldn't control him."

"Precisely," agreed Sir Walter. "Imagine, if you will, the power and cunning of one who has spent his life, his *considerable* life, studying first-hand within the circles of popes, emperors, and monarchs such as those who created this cathedral."

The arc of his gesture took in the whole of the impressive structure, and I felt off-kilter, as if by gazing upward, I receded, grew smaller.

"Imagine such a one without a moral compass beyond the need to dominate others; you already know that he has the ability to avoid undesired confinement; imagine such a one possessed of infinite wealth—"

"Stolen, no doubt," Will murmured.

Sir Walter nodded as he led us back towards the entrance.

"He is protected beyond anything you can imagine by layer upon layer. His ability, he keeps secret from all but his inner circle. You must understand: he terrifies everyone who serves him. He always knows things he shouldn't know about them; though many of his key employees have never seen him in person, yet he knows them intimately. He overhears conversations that he couldn't possibly have been party to. He acts on this knowledge just often enough to keep his employees in abject fear of what he might do or say next."

"He spies on them." Will's voice dripped contempt.

"He is rarely solid," said Sir Walter. "As recently as sixty years ago, he appeared in visible form for an entire day every tenth day. Now, he averages one appearance of three hours only every fifteen and a half days."

"Twice a month?" Will's eyes grew large. "He'll only age three days a year at that rate. For someone who doesn't bat an eye about killing people, he sure is scared of dying."

"Death comes equally to us all, and makes us all equal when it comes," said Mickie. "Pfeffer used to quote that."

Sir Walter smiled. "John Donne. I admired him."

"As in, you knew him?" Will asked.

Sir Walter nodded and made to exit, but before leaving the cathedral, he dipped his hand in the basin to cross himself. Mickie followed suit, and Will, whispering to me that it had been awhile, also crossed himself.

I dipped fingers in the shallow bowl, crossing myself for the first time since Mom's death, and hastily wiped my fingers dry against my jeans. The gesture was hollow: I felt overwhelmed by dark thoughts about Helmann.

Our group re-united outside Notre Dame, and we received a handful of *Métro* tickets for our Paris stay along with our daily five-euro lunch allotment. Then we descended together into the *Métro*, exiting at the Place Charles de Gaulle/Étoiles beside the Arc de Triomphe.

Sir Walter had disappeared at some point, but I'd been pre-occupied with thoughts of Helmann taking over the world, and I'd missed his exit. I recognized an old feeling: the way I could make the outside world muffled and dulled by pulling inside myself. I'd done that for years after losing Mom and Maggie.

Only, I didn't want to live that way anymore. I grabbed for better memories. Me and Will, pounding the pavement early to beat the triple-digit heat of central California. Eating raspberries with Sylvia. Bear hugs from my dad. I found the part of myself that didn't want to go back inside the grayed-out world of my childhood.

I found it and I held on, *tight.*

Taking slow, deliberate breaths, I forced myself to notice my surroundings as students gawked at the Arc de Triomphe. Burning brakes. *Gauloises* cigarettes. Fresh-baked baguettes. It felt cold. Moisture in the air. A steady breeze. Then a wash of warm and sooty air gusted up from a set of *Métro* stairs.

Someone nudged me. Will. "You kind of leave us back there for awhile?"

I lifted my gaze from the scuffed toes of my boots. "A little."

His eyes, dark orbs, held mine.

"But I'm back," I whispered.

"C'mon," said Will. "Let's go see the Eiffel Tower."

"Sounds good," I said.

Will smiled and brushed fingers across the back of my hand as we crowded down the *Métro* stairs once more.

"Where's Sir Walter?" I asked amid the clatter of trains and press of bodies.

"Said he'd meet us at the Eiffel Tower," Mickie replied. "He needed to contact someone about the book."

Once again, I felt a tickle at the back of my mind. *We've got to tell Sir Walter about Helga's book.*

Excerpted from My Father's Brilliant Journey, by Helga Gottlieb

The Experiments conducted by my father during the 1930's and 1940's had a brilliant aim: the creation of a loyal army of chameleons. Some may criticize his methods, and whom better to respond to such a criticism than myself?

As one of his more successful experiments, I can attest that neither harm nor cruelty were inflicted needlessly. The strict regime under which I and my siblings were raised has only served to develop in us the ability to transcend ordinary human limitations. We are hindered neither by weakened emotions nor enfeebled bodies. We are the living proof of my father's genius, should any such proof be deemed necessary.

Some might argue that his methods were crude. Certainly they were at times. It was war time, and in many things my father had to make do with what lay at hand.

But who today could design a more perfect way in which to ensure the indebtedness of one human to another? I still recall from my days of solitary isolation how the man I knew only as Herr Doctor told me I was special. Such words are powerful in a child's growth. With kind attention and with food, he assured my loyalty. I became indebted and remain to this day indebted to the greatest Man of Science the world has known.

Crude his methods may have been; successful they most certainly were.

12

GRAVITY

Upon exiting the *Métro*, we emerged in the shadow of the iconic Eiffel Tower.

"It's freaking huge," said Will.

Beside him, his sister nodded, her mouth falling slightly open.

It was the actual *Tour Eiffel*, just like on the cover of our French book. Our group dispersed—from here we were on our own. We three walked towards the tower, but it was like we never got any closer.

Will grunted. "Food. Smell that? You do the ordering." Will nudged me to a sidewalk *crêperie*.

He was perfectly capable of ordering by himself. But I thought I knew why he'd asked: he wanted to keep me from pulling inside myself again. Warmth filled my belly.

The warm pancake-y scent of the *crêpes*, combined with cheese and maybe something chocolate, intoxicated us. We completely forgot about the Eiffel Tower.

"I want that." Will pointed to a *crêpe* cooking on one of two burners, folded in half with loads of melted cheese, sliced mushrooms and chunks of ham.

I summoned my inner French-girl. When our turn came, Will translated for Mickie, probably intending to annoy her and make me laugh at the same time.

"*Bonjour, Monsieur,*" I said.

("Good day, sir," Will echoed.)

"*Bonjour, Mademoiselle,*" said the *crêpe*-maker.

("He told her 'good day,'" said Will.)

I looked back and caught Mickie rolling her eyes at her brother.

"*Je voudrais une crêpe fromage avec jambon et . . .* Will—how do you say mushroom?"

"*Champignons,*" chorused Will and the *crêpe*-maker.

"*Oui, s'il vous-plaît,*" I said.

("She said, she wants mushrooms, cheese and ham," Will said.)

"Enough, Will, I'm not stupid," Mickie snapped.

I laughed inside, keeping my face directed to the kiosk.

The *crêpe* maker flipped the large pancake over and then in half, dumping a truckload of cheese on top. Will grinned, shooting me a thumbs-up.

After a few minutes we sauntered away with a nutella *crêpe* for me and a *spécialité de maison* for Mickie, which involved strawberries *en flambé*. Mick also grabbed an espresso which came in a dixie-sized plastic cup.

"Looks like mud," said Will.

Mickie smiled and drank it down in two gulps. "Tastes better."

We finished our late lunch; my cell phone informed me that in California, my parents still slept.

"This is too weird," Mickie said, waving her hand at the Eiffel Tower. "Before Sir Walter, I never *imagined* myself coming here, sitting in the shadow of *that*. Not given our . . . realities."

"*La Belle France* is getting to you," Will said, grinning.

His sister merely smiled, too enchanted to bicker. Her realities had been harsh for a long time. Their situation hadn't allowed her even the luxury of pulling inside herself when her mom died. She'd had a kid brother who suddenly depended on her for everything when she'd been maybe two years older than I was right now.

It made my life look easy. It made something bloom inside my heart for her: a soft, warm flower. I shook my head. Mickie wasn't a person you could go around handing soft, warm heart-flowers to.

"Here comes the fourteenth century," Will said.

Mickie back-handed his shoulder. "Will! Keep it down, already."

Definitely not a warm heart-flower kind of girl.

"*Bonjour Mesdemoiselles, Monsieur*," said Sir Walter.

"Was your meeting . . . profitable?" asked Will.

The French gentleman nodded, running his fingers down his pointed goatee. "I have given certain . . . friends . . . a great deal to think over, certainly. I believe things will heat up nicely once the authenticity of the book has been established." He lifted his eyes, studying the *Tour Eiffel*. "And yourselves? You have been to the top already?"

"Actually we just finished lunch," Mickie said. "Some of us can't think without food in our bellies."

"Shut up," muttered Will.

"You want to go up with us?" I asked politely.

"Er, if you will pardon me," said Sir Walter, shaking his head.

"Guess you've had a few chances," Will said.

"No, no, it is not that." Sir Walter looked bashfully at his shoes and then back at us. "I have a most shameful fear of heights."

"That's a common fear," I said.

"For a chameleon, it is a ridiculous one," he replied.

"Why?" asked Mickie, looking from Sir Walter to me and Will.

Will and I shrugged.

"Ah," Sir Walter said. "You have perhaps not experimented as chameleons with . . . gravity?"

Mickie's eyebrows raised. "No, you don't want my brother messing with gravity."

Sir Walter chuckled. "I misspoke. Your brother cannot influence the force of gravity. But a chameleon can operate outside of its influence upon him- or herself."

"Because gravity only affects things that have mass," Mickie said.

Sir Walter nodded but didn't enlighten us further.

"But in our case," I said, trying to draw him out, "We have no mass, right?"

Sir Walter's head inclined once more.

"Okay," said Will, "We give up. How's it work?"

"Let us walk," said Sir Walter. "Unless you would prefer to journey atop *La Tour Eiffel*?"

"Anyone here *have* to go up the tower?" asked Mickie.

We all agreed we could live without going to the top of the Eiffel Tower when the alternate activity was picking Sir Walter's brain for information. We stood to walk back to our hotel, and a bit of late afternoon sun broke through the clouds.

As we strolled along broad boulevards, Sir Walter solved for us the equation of gravity. According to him, moving through air while in chameleon form mirrored moving through water while solid. Essentially, we could

move up and down *through air* as well as up through
ceilings and down through floors.

Will shrugged when I asked if he'd known all this.
"I never tried leaving the ground. I mean, knew about
passing *down* through the floor, but it never seemed
useful to me."

"As with swimming," said Sir Walter, "you *decide*
where it is you wish to go. Although you may upon
occasion observe an unusual effect. If the day is very
blustery, you may find yourself buffeted along *because
you expect the wind to move you.* It is actually within your
choice to move with the wind or not, but sometimes
the mind is influenced into guiding you by the
expectations created by what you can see."

We nodded like this made perfect sense, which I'm
not sure it did, but I just figured I'd stay away from
tornadoes.

"When we have a measure of privacy, I really must
attend to your education as *ree-pillers,*" said our friend,
shaking his head sadly.

A sudden gust of wind, icy, blew past and
passersby bent their heads low, pulled scarves more
tightly.

"Would you prefer a more sheltered journey back
to the hotel?" said Sir Walter, indicating a *Métro*
entrance.

"What, and miss seeing *la Belle France?*" asked
Mickie.

117

Sir Walter chuckled. Will snorted a laugh and flipped his jacket collar up, buttoning it close around his neck.

"I'm fine," I said, pulling gloves on. "It's no worse than back home."

"No offense to *la Belle France*," said Will, "I mean, I'm sure you could tell us lots of stuff about all these buildings, but I've been wondering about the black book. Did the Nazis make Helmann do that stuff to those kids?"

Sir Walter frowned and turned his eyes to the ground. Another gust tossed leaves and bits of paper across our path.

"Alas," said Sir Walter. "No one has forced my cousin to do anything for many centuries. The idea was his alone." Our French friend sighed heavily, leading us onto a sanded path running through a large park.

"His plans have been centuries in the making." Sir Walter broke off as if deciding the best way to present these plans to us.

Clearing his throat, he began again. "Let us suppose you were to offer a group of dedicated followers the possibility that their offspring could live a thousand years as leaders of a new world. I have lived a long while, and believe me when I say to you there are few offers more compelling than the ones promised to your children. This much, my cousin recognized and decided to exploit.

"Because eventually we all realize we will not live forever, and most of us begin to dream of a legacy, a hope that allows us to leave some part of ourselves behind. A great painting, a body of written work or of research, these are the choices of those who eschew reproducing or who have been disappointed in their hopes for their progeny. But the real siren-call has always been that the flesh-of-my-flesh will live on in glory when I am gone."

"Immortality for those not planning on getting into Heaven," said Mickie.

"In a manner of speaking," agreed Sir Walter. "To convince others that he could offer thousand-year-life spans to their children proved impossible in previous ages. I know that he tried during the Napoleonic era; he gave impassioned speeches to select circles about the creation, from their loins, of a new breed of man. But none believed him; thanks to a whispered word here and there, they saw his abilities as the tricks of a charlatan." The old gentleman smiled complacently.

"Thanks to you," I said softly.

He dipped his head in acknowledgment.

"Are you saying back then he was offering to pass out the chameleon gene like candy?" asked Will. "It doesn't make sense. If he made chameleons, how would he possibly control them?" Will asked.

"Jurassic Park," I murmured. "You engineer into the cell a need for something that only *you* can provide.

Something that would cause a chameleon to die without receiving it on a regular basis."

"That's something he could do *now*, but it would have been quite a challenge with earlier technologies," said Mickie. "Although I guess you could have fed them addictive substances."

"Neuroprine was his first modern attempt," Sir Walter explained. "He's spent untold millions upon the problem since then. His bid for power with Napoleon and again with the National Socialists in Germany were but trial runs. He has learned from his mistakes as well as from his successes."

"With all the advances in genetics, and Helmann controlling Geneses, we're talking about something happening within our lifetime," Will said, a grim expression upon his face.

"I should think he will act within the *normal* span of your lives, even," Sir Walter agreed, as though he took it for granted Will and I would choose longer-than-usual lives as chameleons.

"Okay," said Will. "So back up to what you said about proving he could offer long lives to anyone who'd turn to the dark side. Did he make a bunch of chameleons? Was this what he was up to with the children in Nazi Germany?"

"In part, my inquisitive friend," said Sir Walter, looking grave. He sighed heavily. "You have perhaps heard of the *Lebensborn* project?"

120

"Sure," said Mickie. "Himmler's program to increase the birth rate within so-called racially desirable bloodlines. Financial incentives, assistance for wed or unwed blond-haired blue-eyed women who'd become pregnant and provide Aryan children for the Fatherland. Wasn't there something about SS officers having first crack at impregnating volunteers or is that urban myth?"

"It's debated," Will replied.

Sir Walter nodded. "Controversial, yes, but it is fact that Girard gained access to many such willing women in order to reproduce children born with his genetic information. And to make doubly sure, the children were conceived under special circumstances— you recall in my letter that I asked you where Will was conceived?"

"Shelokum Hot Springs in Alaska," said Mickie.

"Dude," said Will. "Enough said. Seriously."

I flushed, thinking about my conception at Bella Fria Hot Springs. Mickie had theorized and Sir Walter had confirmed that along with inheriting the genes to ripple, conception in a hot springs with the presence of gold and tobiasite tweaked the chromosomes to produce the strange genes we carried.

Sir Walter continued. "It is still a mystery why some of his offspring exhibited chameleon-behavior, while others did not. All carried the Helmann's gene, certainly. Pfeffer reported to me that he'd seen documentation of this. Pfeffer said he had a theory of why some rippled and others only experienced numbness. He never told me his idea, and I suppose it perished with him."

"So these kids were ripplers, some of them, and they didn't run away?" asked Will.

"It is, alas, a simple matter to deceive a child—to frighten them from attempting to escape. It was even *true* the children would likely have starved had they escaped. It was wartime and food was in scarce supply."

I shivered. I would have faced starvation, given the choice between hunger and those evil rooms. We crossed a busy boulevard into another park, lush and green even in December.

"Moreover," continued Sir Walter, "as soon as a child could ripple, Helmann began the medicinal treatment which suppressed the ability."

"So, what, Pfeffer didn't take his meds?" Mickie asked.

Sir Walter laughed. "He was even more clever than that. Unlike the other children, Pfeffer never revealed what he could do. I was the first in whom he confided, once he trusted me."

"Sir Walter," said Mickie. "Back to the 'why did some kids ripple' question—Pfeffer said something once."

"Yes?"

"He said that Will would not be who he is without the way our dad treated him while he was *still under the age of eight*. When I asked Pfeffer about it, he seemed upset that he'd spoken aloud and tried to make nothing of his statement. I've been thinking, though, what if the numbness-producing response *changed* to an invisibility-producing response in individuals traumatized prior to a certain age, say, eight years of age?

"As an adaptation, this could exist to give an individual a greater chance for survival. It's well-documented that kids' brains go to a lot of trouble to protect them from the full experience of abuse or torture; kids will report retreating into a mind-space where they 'leave' their bodies while their abusers harm them. When I asked Pfeffer, he wouldn't comment, other than to say it was dangerous to try to learn what I wanted to know."

"Fascinating," said Sir Walter. "Yes, I think perhaps . . . this is most interesting, and disturbing, in light of what we know of my cousin's activities."

"It's true for Sam, too," Mickie said quietly. "She had trauma prior to age eight."

She was right. And some days I still felt like I was recovering from the day I saw my friend and my mother killed.

"Of course, some of the children upon whom Helmann experimented never made it to eight years old. But, yes. Perhaps my cousin intended to traumatize the children with the experiments."

The sun sank behind a thick band of clouds upon the horizon as it hit me what Mickie and Sir Walter were suggesting. All the children upon whom Helmann had experimented, the ones he had traumatized, had abused—they were all his offspring. *His own children.*

This was beyond wrong. My stomach roiled at the thought, and I could not pull my mind back from the horrors of the black book. Once more, words and images from the dark tales rose before me. Hunger. Fighting. The desperate cold. The bowl of poison. All while Helmann stood by, invisibly, taking careful notes.

"Sir Walter," called Will. "Hold up. I think Sam's going to yack."

I barely made it off the sanded path, behind a row of manicured bushes. I fell, gloved hands smacking onto the cold, hard earth, gravel imbedding itself right through my jeans and into my knees. Mickie dropped beside me, holding back my hair. I heaved until my stomach emptied, and then my eyes poured out what liquid remained while Mickie passed tissues to me. It was all too much: the *Lebensborn* children; the experiments in the black book; the cruelty and determination of our enemy.

For the first time, I began to see the full force of what we were up against. How could we possibly hope to prevail?

At last, with Mickie's help, I stood. Before us, the sun settled for the night, a bloated red ball that hovered ominously over the horizon of Paris before giving up at last and vanishing.

"Earliest sunset of the year," said Mickie, quietly.

"Perhaps we have dwelt enough for one day upon the darkness in this world," said Sir Walter, looking sorrowfully my direction. "If you have no objections to the consolations of the Holy Church, we might attend a sung mass."

"We're Catholic," Will said.

Mick made a small noise that might have been a laugh, but she raised no objection.

"My family doesn't really go to mass," I said. "But it sounds fine by me." I thought I could use some *Lord, have mercy* right now.

"Sir Walter, I just have one last question. Sam, do you mind?" Will turned his dark eyes upon me.

"No problem," I murmured. Like I could say no to him.

He turned back to Sir Walter. "The black book, those experiments? It seemed so purposeful, like he was after something more than traumatizing them," said Will.

"Of course, my friend. He broke their spirits in order to train his army," said Sir Walter.

Mickie spoke in a crisp tone. "Enough. We're done for today." Protectively, she placed an arm around me.

All conversation was at an end, and we stood quietly with our own dismal thoughts. Sir Walter conjured a taxi out of a mass of yellow headlights streaming towards us, and we rode in silence to a building marked *Palais de Justice*.

Will took a long, hard look at me as we parked. "Do you want to just go back to the hotel?"

"I don't want to offend Sir Walter," I whispered.

The French gentleman overheard us and chuckled softly. "God cares not, child. Perhaps rest is what you need now, more than the celebration of the Mass."

Mickie and Will exited the cab as Sir Walter spoke to the driver in rapid French. Winking at me, Sir Walter shut the door, my driver departed, and I collapsed once more into the back seat, exhausted. I rested my gaze on shuffling pedestrians as the taxi crept along the boulevard. The traffic reminded me of times I'd visited San Francisco; people on the sidewalks made better time than we could driving in a car. But it felt so good to be sitting.

I watched the faces of the pedestrians moving past. I smiled, imagining the stories Gwyn would make up if she were with me.

If we were friends.

I sighed. Gwyn's voice tickled inside my head. *This guy has to go home and tell his wife they're being relocated to Iceland in the dead of winter; that woman just found out she's pregnant with octuplets; that guy won the national lottery and spent it all on cheap whiskey . . .* I heard her laughter in my head and tried to play the game myself for awhile. But my own mood was too somber. *This girl just found out that there was a dad in World War II Germany who tortured his own children.*

My eyes landed on a burly man with white-blond hair. For the most part, Parisians seemed to be dark-haired, so this guy stuck out. I watched him as he drew nearer, his expression a dour *transferred-to-Iceland.* My taxi driver slowed, causing the brakes to squeal noisily. The pedestrian looked up as he passed us. I twisted away just as he met my eyes, certain of who I'd seen: *the blue-eyed man from Helga's lab—Ivanovich!*

I shrunk down into the seat, fear filling my veins like ice.

He doesn't know you, I said to myself. He'd seen me last with a black nylon stocking that smashed my face beyond recognition. As proof that I wasn't recognizable, he hadn't connected my stocking-ed face with the drawing of me advertising my supposed "lost purse."

But that didn't matter, I realized. He *did* know what I looked like. He might not realize we'd met three weeks ago in Helga's lab, but he knew me as "Jane

Smith," the fake name I'd given the first time I visited UC Merced. And from the poster, he knew his employer wanted me.

I snuck a peek out the back window of the taxi. Would he double back and pursue me? In the deepening twilight, it was impossible to be sure, but I didn't locate anyone with blond hair looking back at my taxi.

I let out a huge sigh of relief.

And then I took in a gasp of air, ready to scream as the man with ice-blue eyes materialized in the taxi beside me.

13

NEEDLES

My scream never came. Before I had a chance, my pursuer threw large arms around me and rippled away, taking me with him. I quickly lost all sense of direction as he began a mad, invisible race through Paris with me locked in his arms.

At first I had no thought of struggling free; the crazy-fast speed at which we moved disoriented me. Then we slowed and dove *underground* passing through floors, rock, soil, and I didn't know what-all. I grew afraid that if I tried to materialize, I would end up doing so within something solid.

Images from his mind flooded into my own. Fearful this could be a two-way occurrence, I focused on preventing him from gaining anything from my mind. I dwelt upon one single image: the WANTED

poster of me with the sticky note reading *Do Not Harm.*
I repeated this single image again and again in hopes
the message might influence my captor.

Overlaying this image of mine, I saw visions from
Ivanovich's mind: Helga in a raging passion, a wall
made of stacked skulls, a row of red-filled vials, a birds-
eye view while skimming over the surface of an
immense lake or perhaps ocean; on and on the images
came in relentless waves—more images than I figured I
probably had in my head over the course of several
weeks. This guy's brain was way too busy.

And then all at once we stopped. I felt my flesh
returning as my captor threw me from himself. I hit the
ground hard and tumbled over, hurtling into a desk.

My weight and speed pushed the desk into
something more solid. A wall? I heard the sound of
things falling to the floor, dislodged by the collision.
From where I lay, I saw what looked like a dog bone
rolling towards me and coming to rest.

I tried to rise, but the room spun wrong-ways-up,
and I shut my eyes tight. As I fell back to the rough
flooring, I hit my head. Stupefied, I lay still. I thought
maybe my head hurt, but then I wasn't so sure. Maybe
it just felt heavy.

"Deuxième's got her, that's right, she's ours now,"
said the man. His voice sounded wrong. I struggled to
work out why.

"Such a deal of blood. So very, very red. But dirty. Not good clean blood," he continued.

I realized he was muttering in French. And he wasn't directing his speech at me. I lifted my head a centimeter to see who else was in this place. My brain tried to make sense of what I could see in the dimly-lit space. Rows of sticks decorating a wall. I squinted, examining the patterns, far more complex than any brick-laying I'd ever seen. And then it dawned on me that I was looking at a wall made not of sticks, but of bones.

He'd brought me into Paris' underground bone-charnel. And there was no one else here.

As he continued speaking, I realized something else was wrong with his voice: it didn't sound like Ivanovich at all, in fact. He spoke in a high pitch with a frantic, breathy quality. He sounded nothing like the man I'd fled in Helga's laboratory, but he looked identical, right down to a dark mole below his left eye.

"It's necessary to be sure; It's necessary to be correct. We can't call *die Mutter* unless we're sure. Check her blood. Check her blood."

He was talking to himself, I realized. As he continued muttering, I kept my eyes pinched almost closed. It felt like it gave me an advantage, although I had no plan at the moment, except to calm my pulse and try rippling.

'Cause that's always worked so well for you when you're scared. I had to face the possibility that I wouldn't be able to find my rippling "zone" here any more than I had in Helga's lab. I wasn't Will; this didn't come to me second-nature.

Deep breath in, slow breath out, I told myself.

"She might wake up. She might not. Let's tie her hands together," continued the voice. "That's a good plan Deuxième, a good plan."

And with that, he seized both my hands and duct-taped them together.

Crap! My heart started pounding again, and my head with it.

"Lots of blood, lots of blood, but it is not clean. Deuxième can't use dirty blood."

I felt a tickle beside my ear as I identified the smell of my own blood. I'd cut something by my ear.

"Can't get a clear look at her now she's got her eyes closed. She needs to wake up. Deuxième has things to make her wake up."

Through squinted eyes, I saw him open a cupboard that appeared to be full of medical or scientific supplies. He located a small vial and then rummaged until he found a needle.

Oh, God! What's he going to pump inside of me?

"She must wake up. This will wake her up." Here, he laughed. It was a childish laugh, and it sent a chill down my spine.

"I'm awake!" I cried out in French.

"American," he said. "She sounds like an American."

I didn't say anything in response. I'd seen a mouse once on television, frozen before a rattlesnake. I knew how it felt to be the mouse now.

"From California. That is where she lives." He stared at me, tilting his head sideways to get a better look at my face along the ground.

"Maybe she will tell us her name."

His icy blue eyes drew closer to mine and I flinched.

"What is your name, girl?"

I said nothing, still thinking about that stupid rodent. I didn't want to be the mouse.

"Deuxième forgets that she is American. Lazy Americans speak only English." These things, he murmured to himself in French. Then, switching to English, he addressed me once more. "What are you called?"

"I'm Jane Smith," I lied, figuring it was safer to stick to that identity than reveal my actual name. "What are you called?"

Here he flashed a grin of polished teeth. "Now I am Deuxième. Later Ivanovich will be here and Deuxième will get to rest."

"You have . . . two names?" I asked.

"Of course," he said, wrinkling his brow. "When Deuxième sleeps, Ivanovich is our name. When Ivanovich sleeps, we are Deuxième."

I nodded as though what he said made sense. It didn't, exactly, but I didn't want to antagonize him. Helga's thug was more than just an *über*-man. He had some form of *über*-multiple personality disorder that she'd employed to her advantage.

"Deuxième needs clean blood," he said, turning back to the cupboard.

As soon as he turned his back to me, I began scooting backwards and away from him towards a low opening in the wall behind me.

He spun back around. "No!" He grabbed me roughly and shoved me down onto a small wooden bench. Grabbing the duct tape once more, he ran it over my lap, securing me to the bench. "Jane must stay here."

His simple speech reminded me of a child.

"I don't want to stay here," I said, adjusting my tone to match his. My voice came out surprisingly calm.

"Sometimes Deuxième is unhappy to be here, Jane. But Deuxième does what he is told. Ivanovich got us in trouble. *Die Mutter* said Ivanovich deserved to be banished. Poor Deuxième had to come here as well."

"Come here from where?" I asked.

He stood, confident that I could not longer escape. He ignored my question as he returned to searching his cupboard.

"From California?" I asked.

"Mmmm-hmm," he said, inflecting the sound just enough that it meant "yes."

"Samples must always be clean. Clean samples yield clear results," he said as he spun back around. In his hands he held two empty vials and a different kind of needle along with a length of rubber tubing.

No, I thought. *Please, no!* He wanted to draw blood. With a needle.

Panic or fainting would take me farther from being able to ripple. Could I distract Deuxième and prevent him from drawing my blood?

"*Deuxième* means 'Second,' right?" I asked.

"Yes," he said as he began tying the tubing above my elbow.

I tried not to stare at the wickedly sharp needle he'd placed on the bench beside me.

"Was there ever a . . . First?" I asked.

He grabbed the needle. His face looked troubled. "He is gone," he said simply. "She destroyed him with too many experiments."

"She did?" I asked.

His hands had stopped their activity and he looked down and to one side.

"Yes," he answered.

"Were there more than the three of you at any time?"

"Just three. Until she destroyed Bruno."

"Why would she do that?"

"*Die Mutter* needed to experiment," he said, frowning at me. "Why else?"

"So he had to die?" I asked. "That must have been terrible for you."

Deuxième looked unhappily at the vials in his hand. "Yes, very terrible. Without Bruno, Ivanovich and I must work longer hours."

"Wait, what? What do you mean *work longer*?" I asked. I was tied to a wooden bench by a man holding a freaking needle; I couldn't run out of questions.

"While Bruno lived, Ivanovich and Deuxième could rest for sixteen hours and work for eight. Now Ivanovich works twelve hours while Deuxième rests and Deuxième works twelve hours while Ivanovich rests." He looked very despondent as he reported this to me, eyelids drooping.

"So one of you is always . . . awake?" I asked.

"The body we share does not require sleep. We are the *über-kinder*, fore-runner of the new man." He didn't sound very excited about this.

"That sounds like a painful life," I said. *My heart rate is slowing,* I thought silently. I just needed to keep him talking.

"*Painful*," he said. "Yes, *pain* is necessary. *Pain* is the great motivator." His eyes fluttered and he seemed to shift into a higher state of alertness with each repetition of the word "pain." He stared at the objects still in his hands and began testing my arm for a vein.

"Good veins," he said, removing a plastic wrap from the needle.

I felt a sick rush of nausea. I'd run out of questions.

"She has very good veins," he repeated, prodding my arm with his fingers.

The room tilted off-center and I watched in horrible, sickened fascination as the needle crept slowly toward my arm.

Finding a vein, he inserted the sharp bright point.

14

THE MOTHER

You will not pass out! I ordered myself. *You will get out of this place in one piece!*

Deuxième dragged the needle tip back and forth trying to insert it into my vein.

I wanted to vomit; I wanted to pass out. But I forced myself to stay clear.

"We can't find it," muttered Deuxième. "Such a good vein and we can't find the entrance." He yanked the needle out in a quick and frustrated motion. Throwing that needle aside, he grabbed another one and ripped off the packaging. "Another try."

My stomach lurched again.

"Deuxième," I said, trying desperately to keep it together as he brought another needle towards me. "Uh, why do you want my blood?"

He drew his lips back from his teeth in a grim replication of a smile. "Deuxième is very good conversing with blood and learning all that it has to tell."

"Oh," I said. "So, you're like, a blood-expert."

"Deuxième is the *über*-expert of blood." He laughed softly to himself.

"So, uh, how did you become interested in blood?" I asked, trying to get the conversation flowing again.

He looked down, a slight frown pulling at the side of his mouth. The hand holding the needle twitched once, twice. "She said we must learn everything that can be learned about a man from his blood or a woman from her blood."

Here he raised and lowered his shoulders in an awkward approximation of a shrug. Compared to confident, crazed Ivanovich, Deuxième was something of a geek.

"So Deuxième studied and studied," he said. "He studies still. He must never cease learning. Knowledge is power. Power is necessary."

I frowned. "She never gave you a chance, you mean. To choose something else to study. Something you might like even more. Deuxième, that is sad."

He'd tightened his grip upon the needle. It broke. He seemed not to notice.

"What must be, is," he said simply. "Deuxième was not created for a wasteful life; Deuxième was created to obey and to serve. Ivanovich serves by protecting *die Mutter*; Bruno served by . . ." Here he drew his brows together considering the answer. At last he spoke. "Bruno was created to discover how far a man can be hurt and still live and serve. Deuxième is fortunate to be, instead, a man of science and discovery."

I felt my skin turn to goose-flesh as the hairs along my arm rose.

"I don't know, Deuxième. It sounds to me like you have no freedom. I wouldn't call that fortunate. You're like, a modern-day slave."

"Yes," he agreed. "We serve."

I couldn't think of how to get past his stubborn acceptance of his lot in life. How do you convince someone to think outside the little box they've always lived in?

"Jane must not talk further," he said, frowning. "Deuxième has a job to do, and Jane is causing him to become inefficient."

"I just want to help you." I said. A note of fear clung to my voice. I wondered if he could hear it.

"Jane is very . . . kind," he said, feeling once more for a vein. "But *die Mutter* is more cruel that Jane is kind. Deuxième must not disappoint her. Deuxième must test Jane's blood."

He looked at me sadly. "*Die Mutter* knows that Jane Smith is not who she claims to be. *Die Mutter* wishes to know who Jane is, truly. Ivanovich collected Jane's blood once, but Deuxième could not use such a filthy, dried-up sample."

He looked now at the broken needle he held, noticing it for the first time.

Ivanovich had collected my blood? I shivered, remembering how I'd been caught by Helga's henchman on my birthday, the first time I'd snuck into her laboratory. Yeah, Ivanovich had collected "Jane's" blood all over his ugly knuckles. *Die Mutter* had to be Helga. She still wanted to know my identity. And I couldn't let her discover it.

My heart began pounding crazy-fast: partly because Deuxième was looking for a needle again, partly out of fear of Helga discovering who I really was. I should have tried rippling earlier while I'd had Deuxième distracted! I was going to pass out. I was going to lose my cover as "Jane Smith." Helga would learn I was a rippler—the very rippler her father desired. And from me, it was only a short step to Mickie and to Will. Fear threatened to consume me.

Deuxième raised the needle, ready to jab me again. But then something deep inside me bared its teeth. *Fight,* commanded a small but insistent voice. *Take the fear and turn it into strength!* A guttural cry broke from deep in my belly, and I lurched forward, the bench

141

flying off the ground because it was attached to me. I swung it from side to side, catching the back of Deuxième's knee. He grunted and fell forward against the cupboard. Turning, I took a run towards the doorway, shouting as I ran.

"I'm sorry, Deuxième!"

There's not enough room, I said to myself. *The bench won't fit through the passage.* I hurled myself at the passage, arms taped together, legs strapped to a bench. It was stupid of me. The wooden seat caught on one side of the bone-wall and I tripped forward onto the ground, the duct-tape ripping painfully free of my legs as I fell.

From behind, I heard Deuxième stumbling towards me, his passage slowed by bones clattering from the damaged doorway. There was a moment's silence, and then I heard the grinding noise of one of the bone-walls collapsing. I threw a glance over my shoulder and saw Deuxième knocked to the ground as the disintegrating wall led the ceiling to cave in. And then the air grew thick with dust and I couldn't see anything more.

Kicking the bench aside, I backed down the tunnel I'd just entered.

"Deuxième?" I called. "Are you alright?"

No response.

"Oh, no," I murmured. "I didn't mean . . ." I broke off, uncertain what I'd meant to do.

You don't know that he's . . . gone, I said to myself. *But you can't stick around to find out, either!*

Nor could I allow him to lie here unaided. I wasn't Helga. I wasn't Helmann. I wouldn't leave a man to die here among the bones. I had a cell phone. I would call emergency services to this location in case he could be saved.

As I walked I used my teeth to tear at the duct tape binding my hands. Holding my shirt to my mouth, I took slow breaths and retreated along a dark pathway, running a hand along one side of the strange wall until the air felt fresher. As I progressed, I saw light. A few steps further and I encountered a metal gate. I tried to open it, but it wouldn't budge. For a moment, courage failed me. Then, blinking back tears, I laughed.

No gate could hold me in.

I imagined the most bliss-inducing thing I could remember: Will's mouth upon mine, Will's arms surrounding me, embracing me.

I no longer noticed the dust and stale air.

The pain where the needle had been inserted was gone as well.

I'd vanished. I passed through the blood-like tang of the iron gate.

As I began to climb stairs towards the surface streets of Paris, my mind brought to me a tidbit of German.

Die Mutter.

It was German for "the Mother." Deuxième, Helga's thug-scientist-human-experiment wrapped into one, was also her child.

15

GWYN

I arrived at the hotel and trudged behind the front desk to the unreliable elevator, praying it would be in service this evening. My legs shook with exhaustion and my head had begun to pound where I'd struck it on the hard floor. If I wrinkled my forehead, I could feel a crusty line of blood now congealing into a scab. Brushing a hand across the wound, I realized that whole side of my face felt bruised; I probably looked awful.

As I stood waiting for the elevator to decide whether it was in the mood to show up or not, I heard a familiar laugh.

Gwyn.

And me looking like I'd just gone a couple of rounds in a boxing ring.

I was in the midst of deciding to take the stairs instead when Gwyn burst around the corner, her ear pressed to her phone. She stopped and noticed me. We stood silent for a moment.

"I'll call you back later," she said, clicking off her call.

I met her eyes, but then I gave up and looked away. She'd misinterpret this just like she had everything else. And I couldn't say anything without putting Will and his sister at risk. Sighing, I attempted to move past her and take the stairs.

"No!" Gwyn's voice echoed up into the twelve-foot ceiling.

I turned back, confused or curious, I'm not sure which.

"This has got to stop. *Now!*" Gwyn's face was white with anger.

"Gwyn," I said, shaking my head. "You don't understand—"

"No, I don't!" she shouted. "I don't understand how someone as intelligent and strong as you can put up with this."

"I'm not—"

Gwyn cut me off. "Not one more minute. You are *done* with him. Do you hear me? I'm calling the police. I'm calling Madame Evans. I'm calling—"

"No!" I cried. "You're not calling anyone. You don't understand the first thing about my life or about Will."

"Oh, I understand plenty!" Gwyn's face contorted with righteous anger. "Everyone says how you never had any friends after I left. We all saw how you hooked up with Will the minute he looked your way. Sam, I *get it:* you were lonely. It felt good to be noticed."

I shook my head in disbelief.

"Some part of you decided you could live with the abuse if it meant you got attention from a guy. But he's not worth it! No guy is. I don't care how gorgeous his eyes are. *He's evil!* And this has got to stop now!"

I didn't know where to start, how to set her straight. But I knew one thing: I would not let her smear the reputation of the most decent human being I'd ever met. I took a deep breath and said, as calmly as I could, "You're wrong."

Gwyn grabbed me by the shoulders, spinning me around until I faced a mirror. "No, Samantha," she said harshly, "*That* is wrong."

I looked worse than I'd imagined.

Besides the injury that had trickled blood along one side of my face, there was a raised ridge over one eye, the skin furiously red. A smudge of dirt gave the appearance of additional bruising under my cheeks. My jacket had torn along the shoulder.

I rubbed at the smudge, watching it fade.

"What did he do?" she whispered. "Throw you down on the street?"

"Will's not the responsible party," I began, but Gwyn interrupted me with a shriek.

"You did not just say that!" She pointed at my face in the mirror. "The hands that did that to you *are responsible*. He's got your mind so warped you don't know up from down, Sam!"

At this moment Mickie burst around the corner, evidently sharing a joke with Sir Walter.

"Will's racing us up five flights of—" Mickie stopped in her tracks. "Oh my God, Sam. What happened to you?"

"What happened?" shouted Gwyn. "*What happened?*"

Gwyn's rant continued as Mickie examined my face, her fingers cool and gentle upon my skin.

"Hello, I'm talking to you!" Gwyn shouted to Mickie.

Mickie turned to Gwyn, as though noticing an annoying fly buzzing around. "I'm sorry, I'm sure whatever you have to say is very important, but it's going to have to wait. Sam's been injured."

Gwyn planted herself directly in front of Mickie.

"No shit, Sherlock," she said. "By your brother. What do you have to say about that?"

"What?" asked Mickie. "Will's been with us. I don't know what you think you know, and honestly I don't care. Sam's my priority at the moment." She attempted to brush past Gwyn and into the elevator, which had finally arrived.

"Stop right there!" roared Gwyn.

Our noise had at last attracted the attention of the clerk at the desk. He rounded the corner just as Gwyn finished shouting. The desk clerk was obviously *not* pleased with any of us.

Sir Walter spoke with him so quickly that all I caught was something about "affairs of the heart." This seemed to satisfy the clerk, who winked at our French gentleman and exited. Sir Walter, directing all of us to *be quiet please,* herded us onto the elevator and pressed the button for the fifth floor.

Gwyn could not contain herself, however, and a shouting match ensued between her and Mickie.

I slipped over to Sir Walter and offered an explanation of what Gwyn thought, and why she thought it, finishing just as the elevator arrived on our floor.

"Ladies," said Sir Walter in a commanding voice. "Silence, please. Samantha's well-being is our priority here. I trust we are all agreed upon that point?"

Mickie nodded curtly and Gwyn opened her mouth to say something, but thought better of it and mumbled a "yes."

"Mademoiselle Gwyn," said Sir Walter, with a tiny bow, "I beg you will excuse us for the time being."

Mickie was shoving me through the door. Inside, Will stood grinning.

"Told you I'd beat you," he said. Then his expression changed. "Sam! What happened?"

Behind us, Sir Walter had succeeded in closing the door on Gwyn. "And now, perhaps *Mademoiselle* Mickie, you might turn your attention to our injured friend?"

"Sam?" Will waited for an explanation.

While Mickie bathed my face with a warm washcloth, I began to explain about my trip to the underground ossuary. I had only gotten as far Deuxième's secret phlebotomy lab when we were interrupted by a knock upon the door.

"Oh, for heaven's sake," said Mickie, rising to answer the door.

Will took over cleaning my face, his touch even gentler than his sister's.

Sir Walter joined Mickie at the door. It was Gwyn. And she wasn't at all concerned with keeping her voice down.

"I demand that you release Sam *this minute*," Gwyn said. "Let her go free or I shout 'til I lose my voice." I could imagine the fire in her black eyes.

Mickie threw her hands up, muttering, "Do we need this? Really?" while Sir Walter beckoned Gwyn.

"Would it please you to join us, *Mademoiselle*?" he asked politely.

"What?" said Gwyn. "Oh. Yeah, why not?" She crossed the room and glared at Will. "You hit her and then everything's fine because you clean up after yourself? Is that how you operate?"

Will's face flushed deep red; it seemed he remembered what I'd told him last fall about Gwyn and her suspicions.

"Okay," I said. "Listen, this has got to stop!"

All eyes turned to me.

Gwyn looked startled but pleased.

I took a deep breath. "Mickie, Gwyn here thinks that your brother and I are together and that he hits me."

Mickie's jaw actually fell open.

"Yeah," I said. "So I need to know what we can tell her so that she stops walking around giving Will the evil eye," I said. "Because I, for one, am not okay with Gwyn thinking stuff like that about Will."

The room fell silent. Sir Walter cleared his throat and we all turned toward him.

"If I might offer a suggestion," he said, his voice quiet and even, "I have always been a proponent of telling the truth."

"You're joking," said Mickie.

"*Mademoiselle Samanthe,*" he said, "Would you say of your friend *Mademoiselle* Gwyn that she is trustworthy?"

"Sure," I said, thinking of all the hundreds of things Gwyn knew of me and had never told anyone.

"But, it's not like it's my call to make. I mean, not *just* mine, anyways."

"I have been a *reader* of personages for a very, very long while. This is a young woman who deserves to hear the truth. And, in fact, it is evident to me that nothing less than the truth will satisfy so true a friend," said Sir Walter, smiling at Gwyn. He then turned his eyes upon me. "If I might have your permission, my dear?"

He wanted to tell her. Well, who better? Maybe he'd thought of a way to explain things without explaining *everything*.

"Be my guest," I said.

Sir Walter cleared his throat and addressed Gwyn. "Your friend Sam possesses genetic material which is highly, ah, *desired* by certain unscrupulous individuals. One of whom has attempted to harm her this evening, if I understand correctly."

I nodded in agreement.

"Would you say that the threat to your person remains immediate?" asked Sir Walter.

"Um," I said, considering how much to reveal. "I'm safe at the moment."

"Excellent," said Sir Walter, turning once more to Gwyn. "As the three of us are most anxious to hear what has befallen *Samanthe* this evening, might I request that you allow her to tell us this without interruption?"

Gwyn crossed her arms and frowned, but nodded her agreement.

I picked up my story from where the man I recognized as "Ivanovich" had abducted me. I didn't mention rippling as I felt a little confused by exactly how much "truth" Sir Walter thought we should be sharing at the moment. I also left out how I'd called emergency services to rescue Deuxième. I didn't think Mick would react really well to that part, and I didn't want to give Gwyn more cause for thinking Will's family members were volatile.

"Did he recognize you?" asked Will when I'd finished my story.

"He recognized me as 'Jane Smith,'" I replied. "He didn't seem to know me as, er, Sam-who-hides-well." I hoped Will understood my reference to the most recent time we'd run into Helga's henchman. Just another thing I had to keep hidden from Mickie.

Gwyn shook her head and sank into a chair. "So you're telling me someone's been trying to kidnap Sam because she's got freaky genes?"

"Yeah," I said. "The same someones who killed my mom and my friend."

"That was a drunk driver," Gwyn said. "An accident, right?"

I sighed heavily. "When I told you about it, I thought it had been an accident. I've since learned that my mom and I were targeted because of my genetics.

When they killed Maggie, they thought they'd killed me."

"And now, with the passage of several years, it appears that Samantha is once again in jeopardy. Only, this time, these same personages wish to take her alive," said Sir Walter.

Gwyn seemed to be considering my story. "What about the bruises on your face the day after your birthday?"

"That was the very day I learned someone wanted me," I said. "The same man who abducted me this evening gave me those earlier injuries."

"Why didn't you just tell me?" asked Gwyn, throwing her arms up in exasperation.

"It's complicated," I said. "Other people's lives are tangled up in this as well." I didn't mean to give anyone away, but Gwyn saw my eyes dart to Will and Mickie as I checked how Will's sister was taking this.

Gwyn's brows drew tightly together as she stared from me to Will to Mickie. Then her eyes flew wide. "Omigosh! It's them! They've got what you've got, too. That's why you guys are hiding from your dad, isn't it? So he doesn't sell you out to the guys using Sam as a punching bag!"

She paced in a tight circle around the sofa and coffee table as we sat in stunned silence.

"So, what is it about your genes? Have you got the cure for cancer or something?" asked Gwyn.

I glanced over to Sir Walter.

"A trustworthy ally is a powerful resource," he said.

He wasn't going to make this easy for me. I would have to decide whether to let Gwyn hear the *whole* truth or not. I turned to Mickie and Will, trying to telegraph, *What do you think?* to each of them. Will nodded and his sister shook her head.

Great.

I looked Gwyn in the eye. I wasn't sure I saw the "powerful resource," but in her wrinkled forehead and worried expression I saw the "trustworthy ally" just fine.

I cleared my throat and spoke. "I can turn invisible."

She stared at me, raised one eyebrow and snorted in laughter. "Yeah, right."

"Hey," said Mickie. "She just let you in on a secret that people have *died* for. Show some respect."

"Women die at the hands of their abusers every year, *in secret*," Gwyn retorted. "If I seem skeptical, it's because what Sam just said is about as likely as me sprouting a pair of wings."

Mickie and Gwyn argued back and forth while Will tidied up his sister's supply of first aid items and rinsed the washcloth now stained with my blood.

And I realized that if I wanted Gwyn to believe me, I was going to have to show her what I could do.

I focused my mind on the sound of the water in the basin, watched as Will wrung the cloth out, bright drops—now clear—scattering on the porcelain. He cranked the taps round and round to turn the water off. I watched his long fingers, the scar that I'd never asked about running along his left thumb. I remembered those fingers upon my face just now. Remembered his hands pulling my face to his when we'd kissed. I sighed, let my eyes fall shut, and I felt my body tumble away from me.

Gwyn interrupted my reverie, shouting in frantic Chinese: *"Wo De Tian A!"*

16

THE MOON AND THE STARS

I may not have known Chinese, but no translation was necessary at this point. Will crossed to Gwyn's side, trying to calm her down. Mickie threw her hands out in an I-told-you-so gesture. Sir Walter smiled and stroked his goatee, looking bemused.

"Come back!" Gwyn's voice came out in a strangled cry. "Make her come back!" she said to Will. "I believe it—all of it. Just make her come back."

I rippled back into my solid form which occasioned another round of frantic Chinese as Gwyn bounced on her toes and flicked her hands like she wanted to shake something sticky off of them.

"That was—" she broke off looking around the room as if the words were hiding somewhere behind the furniture. "That was *wrong*, Sam." She pointed and shook her finger at me. "Don't you *ever* do that again without warning me first."

I didn't have it in me to point out that I had warned her.

"Omigod, omigod, omigod!" She gave her hands a few last shakes and collapsed into a chair beside Sir Walter.

"I should have told you earlier," I said.

"Are you crazy?" asked Gwyn. "I don't want to know this! I mean, I *wanted* to know what was with you and Will, but I'd much rather go back to living in a world where people don't have the ability to—ew!—do that thing!"

"Ripple," said Mickie. "It's called rippling."

"It's freak-o-zoidal, is what it is. But why would someone want to kidnap you?" asked Gwyn, shaking her head. "Oh—wait—they want to use you for secret government work or clone lots of Sams for a drug lord army, right?"

"Something like that," I replied.

"Okay, but what does this have to do with shooting cats?" asked Gwyn. "Are you going to tell me that was the bad guys chasing you and Will?" She wrapped her sweater around her tightly and let out a moan. "Oh, crap—Will, you do this too, don't you? I get it, I get it. You all do this ripple-thing."

Will looked at his sister, who glared at him and shook her head "No!"

"My sister doesn't have the gene," Will said. "The rest of us do."

"Oh, great," said Mickie. "This is just terrific. Could we maybe get the desk clerk back up here and tell him, too?"

"*Mademoiselle* Mackenzie," said Sir Walter, his tone low and soothing, "The time for secrets is passing. It would be well for us to have someone in Las Abuelitas whose eyes are open. Your French instructor says this young lady's mother knows everything that occurs in your small town?"

"Nothing happens in Las Abs without Bridget Li knowing about it," confirmed Gwyn. "But I still don't understand . . . I don't see why you couldn't have just told me it wasn't Will."

"I tried," I said, tears brimming in my eyes. "But I had to keep Will and his sister safe."

"Oh, God, I'm such an idiot. Will, you don't have to ever speak to me again. I'll understand. You, too, Mickie."

"You were trying to protect someone you loved," said Mickie, sighing heavily. "If anyone can understand that, my brother and I can."

"No worries, Gwyn," said Will, holding out his hand. "It's in the past—shake on it."

Sir Walter asked if he might clarify a few things about my encounter with Deuxième.

"Of course," I said, wiping my eyes.

159

"You say that he displayed a completely separate personality? Distinct from the man whom you previously encountered?" asked the French gentleman.

"Yes. In fact, he said there used to be a third, er, *him*. Someone named Bruno who went nuts from Helga torturing him."

Sir Walter nodded thoughtfully. "These are persons with whom I am familiar. I had thought them twins or even clones. So, Helga Gottlieb has been breeding creatures who require no rest, loyal to her alone. Her father would not be pleased to know this."

"That's biologically impossible," said Mickie. "Humans can't survive without sleep."

"I suspect," began Sir Walter, pulling at the hair upon his chin, "That they serve her invisibly for part of each day. That might provide all the rest required by their, that is, by *his* body." He looked up to me. "But enough talk of these evils."

Mickie looked relieved to hear this. "Thank God you got away, Sam," she said.

"It is indeed providential that the chamber collapsed upon your abductor," said Sir Walter. "Nonetheless, I shall be listening for his thought signature."

"You won't let anything happen to Sam, right?" asked Gwyn, her eyes brimming. "You have a plan, don't you?"

Sir Walter smiled. "I have many plans, all of which are directed towards providing safety for your friend, my dear. And now, I believe, it is time for all of you to rest and for me to think. Since I do that best without the demands of a physical form, I shall now *ree-pill*, which will also allow me to more easily 'hear' the thought signature of Helga's creature, should he venture forth." He bowed to Gwyn. "If you will permit me?"

"Uh, totally. I'll just . . . look the other way," said Gwyn. "No offense."

"None taken," said Sir Walter, vanishing from sight.

"Omigod, Sam," said Gwyn. "I think my brain's going to explode. And you say you went down in the catacombs? Did you want to scream or what? You couldn't pay me enough to set foot down there!"

"People get seriously lost in the catacombs," said Will. "There's like, miles of tunnels."

I shuddered, imagining being lost among the bones.

"Okay, enough already with the fear factor," said Mickie, looking severely at her brother. "Sir Walter's right—it is time for Sam to get some rest."

"Of course," Gwyn burst out, running to hug me. "And tomorrow morning, I'll give you a proper makeover to hide the bruises. Better than those crap make-up jobs you did yourself back home."

I laughed softly and squeezed her hand as she said a final goodnight.

Mickie placed a gentle hand at my back and led me to her own room. Carefully, she tucked me into the soft bed under a thick down comforter.

It occurred to me as I lay drifting towards sleep that I'd never told them about the emergency call I'd placed on Deuxième's behalf. How had I forgotten to mention that? *Because you don't want them to know.* I turned over in bed, curling my knees towards my belly. It was the truth. I feared none of them would approve. They'd see it as an act of foolishness, not mercy.

I didn't feel right, keeping something this important from the rest of them. Their voices rose and fell in the sitting room until sometime around midnight, but I didn't get up to tell them what I'd done, and then I fell asleep.

Sometime later, Mickie came in and checked on me, pulling my bedspread over my shoulders. I should have told them about sending help for Deuxième. Guilt settled upon me, a familiar, well-worn garment.

I fell into a hard sleep after that. My dream was a familiar one. Maggie and me in Mom's car, me in my booster-car seat, because at seven, I didn't tip the scale past sixty pounds. Maggie seatbelted, stroking her new kitten. Me wanting to hold it so badly. Maggie agreeing, making me swear to hold tight to the kitten no matter what. The car arriving back on our street and Maggie opening her door.

The noise spooked the kitten, who clawed and bit me. I squealed and released it.

Maggie ran calling for her new pet.

No, Maggie, I wanted to scream. No, Mommy! But I couldn't make the sounds come out. The car seat release baffled me. I heard Harold's car revving up and I clawed frantically at my buckle. Mom shouted and I looked up as the car struck them.

I tried to keep my dream-self from looking over my shoulder to where Maggie and my mom bled. I tried to stop my dream-self from making the horrible call to 9-1-1.

Usually this was the moment I would wake myself, moaning and crying *No!*

Instead, I slept on.

The dream shifted and I huddled in a corner of Dr. Gottlieb's office while she argued with her brother Hans. She sketched a crayon picture of Mom's car and shouted, "See? See? She's right there!" She punctured the paper as she indicated my position in the car. "That's the girl you were after! Now get back there and finish her off before I tell Father."

Hans stuck his tongue out at her saying, "You're not the boss of me, Helga."

She threw a tin cup of milk at his face. "Father always lets you get away with murder, Hans, but not this time!"

"Oh, that's exactly what I'm getting away with," Hans said, white teeth gleaming.

I awoke from the nightmare, drenched in sweat, with the name "Helga" on my tongue.

Mickie entered the darkened room. "You had a bad dream." She sat beside me, brushing hair back off my damp forehead.

"Yeah."

"I have them, too." She handed me a glass of water. "Drink. So you don't fall back into the same dream."

I took the glass. "Does that work?"

"Sometimes." She gave me a crooked half-smile.

I sipped from the glass.

"Sam, you're a remarkable young woman."

Would she be saying this if she knew I might have just saved one of Helga's thugs? I frowned.

"I mean it. You didn't ask for any of this, and you're jumping in with both feet. It says a lot about who you are. I'd do anything to keep Will safe, but I have no choice. He's my baby brother."

I didn't feel like I had a choice either; I loved him.

"I'm covering my butt, too," I said at last.

She chortled. "I know. But thanks." She stood and straightened my covers, bunched into a twisted wad during my nightmare. "There's something else I've been meaning to thank you for. For being such a good friend to Will. A lot of girls would have walked away, written him off after what he did . . ." She hesitated. "Kissing you, I mean."

I flushed. "He told you about that?"

Mickie rolled her eyes. "Yeah."

I could hear his voice still. *I just want to be friends no matter what, okay?*

Mickie continued. "It's not the first time he's acted on impulse. Drives me freaking crazy. But I love him." She laughed softly. "From the moment Mom first placed him in my arms . . . He's the moon and the stars to me, Sam."

I nodded.

"So, just . . . thanks. Thanks for still being his friend."

I held the truth in my hands at last, like a smooth stone I could turn over and over on my palm. Will had kissed me impulsively. I didn't mean the same thing to him that he meant to me. *The moon and the stars.*

A heaviness settled into the deep reaches of my belly. "Everyone does things they regret," I whispered. "I'll always be his friend."

Since that's all I can be.

17

QUEEN OF RELATIONSHIPS

Our third full day in Paris was devoted to all things Museum. After flaky croissants with Nutella, we set off to conquer the Louvre with Gwyn, who made sure I had a decent amount of cover-up on my face. I saw lots of Art. Really. Old. Art. Even the Mona Lisa looked tired behind her layers of glass. I liked the portraits by David; the men and women from the time following the French Revolution looked like they could hop right out of their portraits and join us for a mid-day meal. Of course, some of them might have lunched with Sir Walter back in the day.

Our French friend spent another day away, apologizing to Mickie that he had matters to which he must attend.

"He said he hasn't heard any *thoughts* from Helga's thug, which means we're safe," said Mickie, grinning.

Or does it? I wondered.

For lunch, we shuffled back to the Latin Quarter. It was a University district, and there were lots of cheap places to eat. Mickie insisted we try something besides crêpes, and we settled on a Middle-Eastern restaurant where neither Will nor I could read the menu. We pointed to what other students our age were eating. Mickie got some kind of sausage which she wouldn't eat, and Will ended up with seafood. Gwyn and I had chicken on couscous and it was fabulous. Then, because Mickie was still hungry, we stopped at a *patisserie* for cream-filled delicacies and café-au-laits.

"Ma seriously needs to learn to make these," said Gwyn, holding up the last bite of her pastry. "What's it called again?"

"*Mille-feuille*," I replied. "For the flaky layers."

"Thousand leaves," Will murmured to Mickie, who was trying to work out what "me-foil" had to do with leaves.

Gwyn licked her fingers clean, sighing with content. "Only one thing we can do to top that."

Will's eyes gleamed. "I've been looking forward to the Cluny Museum."

Gwyn rolled her eyes. "Not a chance."

"We've got those worksheets to turn in," I pointed out. The Cluny Museum, our afternoon stop, held all-things-medieval, and we were required to visit it.

"Ah, but that is where our delightfully geek-ish friend Will comes in," said Gwyn. "Who, I might add, just volunteered to enjoy it on our behalf while you and I indulge in pedicures."

"*Pedicures*?" I asked. "Gwyn, we're in *Paris*."

"What, they don't have toes in France?" she asked.

"Go," said Mickie. "Will's going to be impossible at the Cluny. He'll be spouting about how Sir Walter used to kneel at altars just like the one behind the rope, or how the tapestries were probably sewn during the Papal Schism."

"Woven," said Will.

Mick looked at him blankly.

"Tapestries were woven."

Mickie's eyelids dropped to half-mast. "See what I mean? Go do your pedicures. You can copy off Will when we get back to the hotel."

"You're the worst chaperone ever," I said, squeezing Mick's hand.

Gwyn and I hurried back along the busy boulevard to our hotel.

"I bought these amazing colors at this little shop in Amboise," said Gwyn. "They change color. You know, with your mood."

"I've heard of that," I said.

Gwyn rolled her eyes. "Yeah, it'll be all the rage in Las Abs in about, oh, five years."

We entered the hotel and greeted the desk clerk. As we rounded behind him to the elevator, we both felt a moment's awkwardness, recalling our shouting match here last night.

"Have I apologized in the last hour?" asked Gwyn.

"Hmm, I don't think so." My lips twitched as I tried not smiling. "Whenever you're ready."

"*Je suis désolée,*" she murmured.

The elevator arrived.

"Has a nice ring to it in French," I said, stone-faced.

"In *French,*" huffed Gwyn, "You're required to say '*de rien.*'"

"Maybe next time," I said.

We reached the fifth floor.

In Gwyn's modest hotel room, we washed and loofah-ed our feet. I couldn't remember the last time my toes had seen daylight for this long. Chipped polish clung to several of my toes.

Gwyn chattered away about things back in Las Abs, who'd dumped whom just before Christmas to avoid buying an expensive gift. As I brushed polish on her toes, I relaxed back into the contour of our old friendship. Gwyn could carry both sides of a conversation with anyone nowadays, but I still remembered a time she'd been timid—the day that had cemented our friendship.

In second grade I'd punched a bully in the stomach for calling Gwyn "slanty-eyes." Of course, the bully had his revenge. All the next week, he'd pretended to see my mom's ghost.

"Did you see her? Did you see her?" He would stare, wide-eyed, pointing.

"Where?" I would ask every time, aching inside.

After a few days, he'd told me he was making it up. "Your mom doesn't even care enough to haunt you."

I'd punched him again.

Gwyn's voice brought me back to the present. She stared at me with eyebrows raised. Awaiting an answer.

"Sorry, I missed the question," I said, finishing the second coat on her toes.

"Liar," Gwyn growled. "I'll ask Will if you don't give me an answer."

"Ask Will what?"

"Honestly, Sam." She sighed in exasperation. "Will. You. Dish me the dirt on you and Will," said Gwyn.

I studied the chipped polish on my toes. Bright orange. A remnant from Halloween.

"So?" she asked.

"We're friends." The words stuck in my throat.

"Friends! Hang on while I text CNN with the breaking news." She shook her head and reached for my left foot.

"We *are* friends."

She rubbed polish remover over the chipped orange. "And you, I take it, still want more."

I picked at the polish on my other foot.

"Well, who wouldn't," she said. "He's gorgeous, he loves to hang out in stuffy old museums, and he's got freaky genes. What's not to love?"

"Shut up," I said, a hint of a smile forming upon my face.

"Sam, I am the Queen of Relationships. You can tell me anything."

I sighed as she set down my left foot, beckoning for my right.

"It's hopeless," I said.

"*Queen* of Relationships, Sam. If it's broke, I can fix it. Give me something to work with here."

"Wouldn't that make you the Doctor of Relationships?"

"No, Queen is fine."

"Or the Plumber of Relationships?"

"Okay, if my polish weren't still wet, I would so get up and kick your despondent butt." She glared at me. "Come on, Sam. Nothing's hopeless."

Tears hung on my lower lids. "I think this might be." The words came out in a whisper. I told Gwyn

171

how Will had kissed me last fall. How he'd back-pedaled almost before my lips had dried. How he just wanted to be friends.

Gwyn shook her head as she applied my final coat. "Boys are dumber than a box of rocks."

I laughed in spite of my tears. "A box of rocks?"

"Something Ma's aunties used to say. Maybe it's Confucius." She stared at my toes. "Oooh, they're changing."

My toes were, indeed, changing color. "What's pinky-lavender?" I asked.

She read a small typed sheet that had come with the lacquer. "Pink is 'lucky in love,'" she said. "Well, that's hopeful. For you anyway." Her own toes looked blue.

"What's blue?" I asked.

"Passionate." She frowned. "Green is 'devoted lover,' and purple is 'blessed by your lover.' What happened to angry, excited, happy, and sad?"

"This is France," I said, shrugging.

"Yeah, I guess. Paris, city of love and all that."

"I think it's the City of Light, actually."

She shook her head at me. "Everyone knows Paris is the city of lovers. And you need to show Will a little pink nail polish tonight, okay girl?"

"You want me to take off my shoes for Will?"

"No, dweeb. I meant you need to help him realize he's 'lucky in love.'" She giggled. "Removal of clothing is at your discretion."

A loud knock sounded on Gwyn's door.

"Ask who it is first," I said, a prickle running along my spine.

"It's us," said Mickie's voice.

Gwyn opened the door.

"Just checking to make sure everything's good with you," said Mickie. Her eyes dropped to my new toenail polish. "Nice shade of blue."

Gwyn giggled and I felt my cheeks burning as Will came into the room

"Did I say something wrong?" asked Mickie.

Excerpted from My Father's Brilliant Journey, by Helga Gottlieb

During the setbacks suffered by my father in the nineteenth century, he came upon what would be a breakthrough in the creation of the New Race of Mankind. In this journal entry made in 1812, we see the exact moment—the birth, as it were, of a phoenix from the ashes of my father's despair:

The Emperor is a fool. They are all fools. Napoleon's plan to take the Russian wasteland will destroy him, and France with him.

But does he listen to me? Bah – the fool. He hears only the voices of those who worship him, which I will never do. Let Napoleon be to me as one already dead. I will raise up another leader, one more worthy of my Great Plan.

Not for Napoleon's glory do I labor and study.

My studies. Alas, I remain vexed regarding my researches. Why will the secret of my ability as a chameleon not divulge itself to me? Why could Elisabeth not bear me a child who lived? I still see in my mind's eye the row of five tiny graves. What fault lay in her? None of my children by other women show any sign of extraordinary ability, either. I must continue to seek a woman whose blood runs as true as my own.

And perhaps I was a fool to disregard the words of Waldhart's mother. The Well; always with her it was the Well of Juno.

18

JUST FRIENDS

Our toes fresh and beautiful, Gwyn and I joined our group for an hour-long boat ride on the Seine River. Which basically meant freezing our butts off to see famous buildings lit up at night. Another group on board had booked a champagne-cruise, creating confusion when students accepted tiny flutes of bubbly. Once the chaperones caught on, it became Mickie's job to make sure no one drank any.

I stood with Will on one side and Gwyn on the other as the Eiffel Tower came into our sight-line. Just then, twinkle-lights began dancing up and down the landmark tower. Everyone sighed. I watched as couples around us succumbed to the romance of Paris by night.

"I'm getting pictures," Gwyn said, winking at me and then leaning in to whisper, "City of Love. Think

Pink." She pushed through lip-locked teens to the edge of the boat.

But watching others kiss didn't make me feel boldly romantic. Just a little embarrassed.

"Let's move," I said to Will. We wriggled through flashing cell phones, cameras and lovers to the empty side of the boat.

"Sir Walter told Mick where we'll be spending Christmas," said Will.

"Oh yeah?"

"Carcassonne. It's south, pretty much on top of one of those red dots," Will said.

"I wonder if he's got family in the area."

Will shook his head. "Mickie asked him did he have anyone . . . left."

I looked up, curious.

"The short answer's no, but he told us some family history you should hear. He had this cousin besides Helmann, when he was a kid. Elisabeth de Rocheforte. And he loved her, but she married Girard—Helmann—who treated her badly, and eventually she fled him, moved to a French settlement in Arcadia."

"That's Canada, right?" I asked.

Will nodded. "Walter had hoped she'd come to him, but she refused. She said stretching their lives was wrong and unsatisfying and that she was done with it. In Arcadia, she had another man's child and was pretty much his wife, outside church law. Sir Walter's always kept an eye on her descendants, who were eventually kicked out by the British—"

"And resettled in Louisiana," I said—I knew that bit of history.

"Yeah, actually," he said, looking at me with respect. "The Cajuns. So finally Sir Walter saw her descendants dwindle to where he knew of only one girl left, a twelve-year old named Sophie-Elisabeth. He often visited her family in the U.S. He adored her. This past year, she died after participating in the program that killed all those Helmann's carriers back in the U.S."

"He must have been heartbroken."

"Well, that, *and* mad as hell," Will said. "It's what tipped the scale for him. He'd already been upset about Pfeffer going missing, but the girl was the last straw. She'd reminded him so much of his little cousin."

The lights on the Eiffel Tower stopped sparkling, and our fellow passengers murmured a collective sigh of regret.

"It must be lonely for him now," I said.

"We didn't discuss that. But I think he really enjoys having Mick to talk to."

"And you," I added.

Will's eyes focused on a euro coin he'd pulled from his pocket. He studied the coin as though it were the most interesting thing he'd ever seen.

I wished he'd look at me like that. A wave of sorrow flowed through me and I trembled.

"You're cold," he said. He moved to close the space between us, put his arm tight around me.

It wasn't the cold of the night that chilled me, but I let him think he'd guessed right. I turned my face into his jacket, so he wouldn't see my tears. The pine-y smell of our California home clung to his clothes, and I saw me running beside him in the hot sunshine of a less complicated life.

***

The following morning, our last in Paris, about half of our class left for an optional day-trip to Versailles. Over breakfast, Gwyn begged me to come along.

"Le Petit Trianon, you know, where Marie-Antoinette hooked up with her lover," she said. "It'll be so romantic." She raised an eyebrow and tilted her head to Will, in conversation with his sister.

"Some people would see Marie-Antoinette as a symbol of tragedy, not romance," I pointed out.

Gwyn rolled her eyes, murmuring. "This is why *I* am the Queen of Relationships and *you* are not."

"I can't go. Sir Walter has something instructional planned for us," I said. "I could ask him if you can come, too."

Gwyn shuddered. "I've learned enough from Sir Walter, thank you very much."

As we rose to part, Gwyn hugged me and whispered, "I love Will and Mick's uncle, but I don't think I can take any more new information at the moment."

I smiled. "Enjoy Versailles for me."

Seeing as we'd spent two days in the Loire Valley *châteaux*, I didn't mind missing the palace of the Sun King. I figured anything Sir Walter had planned would be a lot more educational.

Of course, the French gentleman's idea of educational sometimes differed from ours.

"C'mon, Mick, where are we going?" Will must have asked fifteen times in the last half hour since we'd jumped on something called an RER train to meet Sir Walter at a location he'd revealed only to Will's sister.

I'd figured it out but kept my mouth shut.

"I've said all I'm saying on the subject," Mickie replied.

"Yeah, and it was *so* helpful. Seriously, when did Mom say anything about wanting to take us somewhere in Paris?"

Will's grumbling made his sister smirk.

The RER train slowed into its terminal stop, Marne-la-Vallee, and I wondered how long it would take Will to figure out where we were headed. The *Parc Disneyland* signs on the platform did the trick.

"No way! Seriously? Disneyland?" Will whooped and swung his arm in a wide arc over his head. He looked like a six-year-old jacked up on too much Halloween candy. We drew stares from sedate Parisian families as we exited the train station.

"Took you long enough," said his sister. "Guess I shouldn't have dropped you on your head so often when you were little."

Will hugged his sister, lifting her off the ground, ignoring her insults and protestations.

Sir Walter greeted us at the foreground of the park and ushered us through a discreet side-entrance to the front of the Space Mountain line. The man had connections.

We hurtled through space briefly experiencing zero-gravity and g-forces my stomach doesn't want to remember. I know we corkscrewed once, and I'd swear we hung upside down several times before the minute-long adventure concluded in a blur of swirling lights and sparks.

The harnesses retracted and Will jumped out of the seat. I followed slowly, and Mickie looked glad to accept a hand from a cast-member. Beside her, Sir Walter exited with dignity and a tiny smile.

"That was freaking amazing!" Will shouted. "I wonder what it would be like to ride it without the shoulder harness?"

"Lawsuit-in-a-box, idiot." Mickie's color was returning along with her sarcasm—both good signs.

We rounded a building and *Buzz Lightyear Laser Blast* came into view.

"A targeting ride?" asked Will. "Mick, you're going *down!*"

An animatronics Buzz Lightyear greeted us. You haven't lived until you've heard Buzz declaiming against the Evil Emperor Zurg in excited French. Mickie laughed until tears squeezed out the corners of her eyes.

I whispered to her as she slipped into the vehicle with her brother, "Aim for the 'Z's' in circles."

I'm good at the game from annual visits to Disneyland in California. I scored well. But Sir Walter, who rode with me, wiped all of us off the map. He *never* missed what he targeted.

Will was pretty pissed when he learned he was supposed to aim for the "Z"'s and not merely the creatures. "You could have told *me* before the ride started," he said, scowling.

I just smiled.

"I wish the real bad guys went around with the letter "Z" tattooed on their foreheads," Mickie said. "That would come in handy."

"Let's go check out the dungeon," Will said, pointing to the pink castle, oddly elongated compared to the one I knew in California. "Says there's a dragon inside." He tapped his map.

We found the animatronics dragon in a dark cavern lit with a greenish glow.

"He's chained, poor guy," Will said, pointing at a collar. As if in response, its gold-green tail flicked sadly.

Sir Walter leaned toward us. "Here we have a visual metaphor for my cousin's creations," he murmured, pointing to the dragon.

"Dragons?" asked Mickie. "Not seeing it."

"Oh, not actual dragons," said Sir Walter. "But the creatures he bred in dark places, tormented as with these chains . . . there is a certain similarity. To have ensured the loyalty of the *dragonlings* in spite of their incarceration—that was his triumph."

"That was Stockholm Syndrome," said Will. "The bulk-size version."

Mickie shook her head. "Well, it didn't work on Pfeffer, 'cause he hated Helmann."

"For which we can be thankful," said Sir Walter, bowing his head in acquiescence.

"Can we go get some food?" Will asked. "This dragon light makes my stomach hurt."

"Everything makes your stomach hurt," muttered Mickie.

Sir Walter directed us to the restaurant inside the *Pirates of the Caribbean* attraction where we parked ourselves at an island-themed table. As I translated the menu for Mickie, my mind wandered to the black book we'd given Sir Walter: to the section where Helmann described a military school to a young Helga.

"Sir Walter, is the . . . military-school-thing being repeated at Geneses?"

"No, no," he replied. "The work at Geneses is, in large part, exactly what they portray to the outside world: genetics research. Of course, the research will be put to rather different purposes than the ones they advertise."

Our food arrived, halting our conversation.

As the Caribbean-costumed server departed, Mickie asked, "So who's in charge at Geneses?"

"My cousin," replied Sir Walter. "Not officially or under his true name, but his monarchy is absolute."

"What about your cousin's kids?" asked Will. "Are his four 'favorites' still around?"

Sir Walter frowned. "The four I spoke of serve him still. Perhaps you can guess as to their names?"

"Fritz, Hans, Helga, and Franz," said Mickie without batting an eye.

"Precisely," said Sir Walter. "At the moment, however, Helga has been demoted from those who hover in his immediate circle."

"She's got Pfeffer's old lab," said Will.

"Are you sure she was demoted by being placed there?" Mickie asked. "I mean, wouldn't Helmann want Pfeffer's lab turned upside down by someone he trusted?"

"Certainly, but that could have been accomplished by those whose skill sets are very different from Helga's. I consider his demotion of Helga as a mistake most fortunate for us. For decades she enjoyed his favor as the most highly placed member of his personal security detail and a chief assassin. And a more clever or heartless one, he could not have hoped for." Sir Walter paused. "She has considerably less power at the moment. Especially since *Mademoiselle Samanthe* so cleverly dispatched her bodyguard." He smiled at me.

Or possibly saved his life, I thought to myself.

I pushed food around on my plate, appetite gone, sure it must be obvious to everyone at the table that I was hiding something. *I really should tell them what I did.*

But not right now.

"So, out of curiosity," I began, "Why Disneyland today, Sir Walter? I'm glad we're here, but aren't there more important things we could be doing?"

The old man looked thoughtful as he set down his fork and knife with a precision only the French could master. "Do you know the play *Hamlet*, by the English poet?"

"Shakespeare? Sure, we know it," said Will.

"Speak for yourself," Mickie muttered.

Sir Walter smiled. "I shall remind you of a line penned for Hamlet's father, who tells Hamlet, 'this visitation is but to whet thy almost blunted purpose.'"

Mickie snorted. "I'll need that in plain twenty-first century English."

"Hamlet needed a reminder from his father to do what he already knew was right." Sir Walter frowned. "When I have been tempted to walk away from the fight against my cousin, I visit this place to sharpen my resolve."

"Not making the connection *at all*," said Mickie, echoing my own thoughts.

"Look around you," he said. "Of what is this place most full? Children. For whom do I labor? Well, for the good of humankind, no doubt, but that is so vague a concept as to be useless to rouse an old man like myself. No, it has always been for the children that I find myself able to act. For the sake of the descendants of my sweet Elisabeth, who are no more, as well as for those who *do* live, but who will not know a tomorrow if I stand by and do nothing." He paused, eyes moist with unshed tears.

"Sophie-Elisabeth loved the Disney Parks in Florida. I spent many happy days there with her family. And so I come here to remind myself that the world is still a place of merriment, of smiles, of children who deserve a future."

"Hear, hear," said Will, after a long silence. "Let's jump on some rides, watch some little kids having fun."

"Will," muttered his sister, "Grow up."

"All's I'm saying is, we're in freaking *Disneyland Paris,* you know?"

Mickie's glare softened into a smile. She tousled her brother's hair. "So, how do you say 'Arrrrrrgh' in French?"

For Sir Walter's sake, or maybe for Will's, I tried to enjoy the *Pirates* ride, but the skeletons drinking wine that would never assuage their thirst? I couldn't stop thinking about the children in long-ago Germany, dying as their own thirst drove them to taste poison.

19

BAD GUY RADAR

That evening, Sir Walter, Will, Mickie, and I strolled along the Seine as we walked from the *Métro* stop to our hotel. The water roiled, murky and dark. My thoughts felt similarly muddied. I still wondered if I should I tell the *whole* story about my encounter with Deuxième. But I didn't want Mickie blowing up at me for being a soft-hearted idiot who sent help to Helga's thug. So I kept quiet.

"We should probably turn up from the river to get to our hotel," said Will. It was like he kept a GPS in his head, the way he always seemed to have a sense of where he was.

"Not for another two streets," said Mickie.

Sir Walter seemed lost in his own thoughts, his eyes barely open as he walked beside us.

I looked from Will to Mickie to see who would back down this time.

"Suit yourself," Will replied, a half-smile tugging on one side of his mouth.

I thought Will was probably right, but I didn't mind spending a few more minutes alongside the river. In my head, I carried the tune of a French song Mom used to sing to me about a bridge. Maybe it was one of the bridges I could see right now; there were so many in Paris.

We turned up a narrow road flanked by tall apartments, and Sir Walter frowned, finally taking note of where we walked. "I apologize for my absence of mind. We should have turned two streets ago."

Will smirked but said nothing.

"I believe, although I am far from certain, that I have caught an echo of our acquaintance *Monsieur* Ivanovich. It may be he managed to escape with his life. Would you perhaps excuse me for a moment? His thought signature is far easier to catch when I am without substance. Shall we meet back at the hotel?"

"Sure, no worries," Will replied.

Mickie's mouth turned downwards and deepened into a scowl as Sir Walter's form vanished. "Easy for you to say," she muttered.

"Nothing's going to happen, Mick. Sir Walter's on it. He said Ivanovich fears him," said Will. "Although we should have asked him how to get back to the hotel."

Grumbling, Mickie produced a map from her back-pack. Will strolled ahead to look at a parked vespa with admiration. He turned back to me, grinning.

"Now *that* is the way to get around in France," he said.

I shrugged. It looked dangerous to me; I'd nearly been clipped by cars several times in the past day and a half. Madame Evans told us drivers only had to miss pedestrians by one meter, and I was sure some of them made a game of it.

As I strolled closer, Will whispered to me. "Of course, if Mick hadn't declared an elevated security level at the moment, it would be a lot more fun to race around Paris rippling."

I smiled. Will's sister had begged him to stick close and not take unnecessary risks after my encounter with Deuxième. "It would be fun," I agreed.

"We could climb the Eiffel Tower for free, you know," said Will.

"Or get closer to the Mona Lisa," I offered.

"Or maybe—" Will's words were cut short by a gasp from his sister.

Mickie pointed to the opening down one side of the street. "I saw him! At least, I think I did. Big guy? White blonde hair?"

Will looked down the alley, his eyes squinting. "How'd he dig himself out of the catacombs?"

"Sir Walter *just said* he heard his thoughts being broadcasted," said Mickie, gazing uncomfortably down the road. "Let's get over to a busier street."

The side street down which we walked was deserted; suddenly it felt unsafe.

"This way," said Mickie, pointing to our right. "There's a larger street this direction."

Together we headed for the busier thoroughfare.

Whoever Mick had seen, I hoped it wasn't Ivanovich; I wished Sir Walter would come back.

As we turned onto the boulevard, a few tired-looking pedestrians strolled along the far side of the road.

"That's better," murmured Mickie.

Will walked beside us, looking over his shoulder every few seconds.

"I'm sure it's fine, Will," I whispered. "Even if he survived, he's not the only blond guy in Paris."

Will's brows were pulled together in concentration. Overhead, the light continued to fade from dusk to night. I looked from side to side, my own heart beating faster as we continued without Sir Walter reappearing. Could Deuxième have survived the collapse of that room? I'd heard the sirens wailing as they headed toward his location. My heart felt torn; I didn't want to be responsible for his demise, but my life would be a lot easier without him following us.

"Dammit!" Pushing past us and into a sheltered alcove, Will called to us, "It's him. I'm on it!" And with that, Will rippled.

Beside me, Mickie growled. "Idiot, idiot, idiot!" She looked frantically about us for any sign of Will or our pursuer.

I grabbed her hand. "Keep walking. Let's just get back to the hotel."

The boulevard was emptying as we pushed farther along. I felt exposed. Mickie dropped my hand to fumble inside her purse.

"Where is it?" she murmured.

"What?" I asked.

"Mace, I think. Some kind of spray I bought off a guy at a flea market here."

"I think that's highly illegal in France," I said.

Mickie shrugged her shoulders. "So is kidnapping a sixteen-year-old girl out of a taxi."

I balled up my hands into fists and began walking faster towards the hotel.

"There!" Mickie cried.

"What?" I didn't want to hear the answer.

"Bleach-head," she replied.

We peered into the gloom of the darkening road.

"At least I thought I saw something . . ." She broke off but began jogging, pulling me along.

A car brushed past us, two young men making the local version of cat-calls as they sped by. And then I saw him.

Ivanovich raced towards us, Will materializing just behind him in hot pursuit.

"Will!" called Mickie.

Helga's tall thug turned into a side street ahead of us with Will on his heels. As we ran to catch up to them both, Mickie called to her brother using a variety of spicy expletives. We reached the alley, but it was empty. Our eyes adjusted to the shadowy dark of the tiny opening. A dead-end.

Will and our pursuer were nowhere to be seen.

Mickie cursed again.

"Come on," I said, backing out of the alley. "Let's get out of here. We can't help Will if we can't find him."

Mickie mumbled indistinctly, probably additional insults directed at her brother, and tiptoed a few feet farther into the cul-de-sac. "*Will!*" she called. "Ripple back, you troll-spawn!"

"Come on, Mickie," I called in a whisper. "There's no one here." A shiver ran along my spine as I spoke.

"Just another quick sec," said Mick as she ran a couple doors further down the alley.

My forehead wrinkled with worry. I wished Will would stop trying to play super-hero.

"No one's here Mickie," I said again. "They're long gone."

Mickie turned back towards me, a defeated look on her face. I gave her a half-smile and was about to say something comforting when I saw her eyes grow wide with fear.

Looking over my shoulder, I saw Helga's blond henchman barreling towards us from across the busy boulevard. He paused mid-street as an angry motorist swerved, shouting French curses at him.

Mickie spoke one word to me, over her shoulder: "Run!"

Then she flew towards the blond man, waving her arms and shouting at the top of her lungs.

20

PAYBACK

"No!" I called as she ran towards the angry man. I dashed after her, my legs pumping crazy-fast. She didn't have that much of a head start, but I tripped on the irregular surface of the old street and tumbled down, catching myself with my hands.

Raising my head, I watched as something truly bizarre unfolded thirty feet ahead of me. The tall blond man seemed to alter his appearance as completely as possible. His face, which had been twisted with determination, softened and calmed. The mouth that had bared fierce canines a moment earlier relaxed. His shoulders slumped forward, and he seemed to shrink in stature as his gait loosened. Hands that had been clenched in tight fists now uncurled and dropped nonchalantly into his pockets.

He had transformed from a raging fiend into a man without a care in the world. I felt like I'd just watched the Incredible Hulk turn back into a mild-mannered scientist.

"*Of course,*" I whispered. I had just seen Ivanovich check out for the night and Deuxième come on duty. "Deuxième?" I called as I stood.

Mickie got there moments before I did. Deuxième looked past her at me and then pulled one hand out of his pocket. In the three seconds that it took me to reach him, he grabbed Mickie, pushed up one of her sleeves, and injected her with something. She slumped immediately into his waiting arms.

"No!" I cried. "What are you doing?"

"This way," he said in English, gesturing towards the alley I'd just left.

"What have you done to her?" I called out, following him into the enclosed street.

"She will be fine," he said. "It is a short-acting sedative. She'll awaken in another two minutes."

"What do you want?" I asked, backing away from him.

"Deuxième wishes to speak with Jane Smith," he said simply.

"What did you have to go drugging her for?" I asked, my voice sounding angry.

He looked bashful. "Deuxième is sorry for harming Jane's friend. Jane's friend will have a bad

195

headache when she awakens." He fumbled around in one of his pockets and withdrew a small vial.

Instinctively, I jumped back.

"This will take away her pain. Deuxième compounded it himself." He looked pleased with himself. "It is very strong medicine for pain."

I took the small vial, doubtful Mick would accept treatment from such a source.

He continued. "Deuxième reasoned that if Jane would send help to a stranger such as Deuxième when he was injured, then Jane is not someone to run away if her very special friend is unconscious."

I screwed my mouth into a tight knot and glared at him.

"*N'est-ce pas?*" he asked in French: *Right?*

"Of course I won't run off with M—" I snatched back her identity as it dangled, caught in my throat. "With my friend in that condition. So spit it out. What do you want?"

At that moment, Will rippled solid at the mouth of the alley. Swearing, he ran towards his sister and her captor, roaring like a wild thing. "Let her go this second," he shouted.

Deuxième retreated. "Stop or Deuxième vanishes with Jane's friend," he said to Will.

Will hesitated.

"That was a good trick you showed Ivanovich," he said. "Ivanovich shared it with me. Now Deuxième knows how to take someone away with him when he vanishes."

Will cursed.

In Deuxième's arms, Mickie moaned softly.

"Deuxième means no harm," he said, stifling a yelp as Mickie, coming around, attempted to escape by *biting* her way free.

"So let her go," said Will fists clenching and unclenching.

Deuxième shrugged. "Deuxième will do so after he has delivered his message."

"How about you let her go *now*," said Will, his dark eyes flashing dangerously.

"Let him talk, Will," I said. "What do you want to tell us?"

"Deuxième is behaving very, very badly today," he said, doubt furrowing his forehead. "But Deuxième wishes to repay a debt. Ivanovich will be angry . . ." He hesitated.

"Out with it, already," shouted Will, barely able to contain his rage at seeing his sister struggling in Deuxième's arms.

"It is a message for Jane," said Deuxième, wincing again as Mick kicked his shins. Deuxième hoisted her into a more secure position over his shoulder. She screamed in outrage.

"Deuxième, can you please put her down?" I asked.

"Does Jane promise to listen to Deuxième?" His hands were still preoccupied with a very enraged Mickie.

"Just tell me what it is you want to tell me," I said. "I will listen."

"Deuxième thought Jane might run away without this one to stay for," he said, tilting his head to Mickie.

"I won't run away," I said. "I promise. Just, please, let her go and tell me what you came to tell me."

Carefully, Deuxième set Mickie down as if she were made of porcelain. She got in one last kick to his shins and ran to her brother, placing herself slightly in front, guarding him.

"It is about *die Mutter*," said Deuxième. He had grabbed one hand with the other and now wrung them together, his distress palpable. "She will be very angry if she knows Deuxième warned you."

"Warned me about what?" I asked.

He dropped his eyes to the ground, shaking his head from side to side. "Very angry. Very, very angry."

Slowly, I walked closer to Deuxième. "Your head," I said, pointing to a butterfly bandage. "You were injured when the roof collapsed."

"Sam!" called Will. "Stop right there!"

"It's okay," I said. I crept a few steps closer. "I'm sorry," I said. "*Je suis désolée*," I repeated in French.

He switched to French as well. "She wishes to use you, Jane Smith. *Die Mutter* believes you are special. She believes you are unique. She believes that if you were to have offspring they would make better servants than poor Deuxième and Ivanovich."

I recoiled. *This was what Helga wanted me for?*

"Sam," called Mickie. "Please, back away!"

"It's okay," I said, hoping I was right.

"She wishes to capture you. Even though her father has forbidden it. Please, Jane Smith, be careful. Ivanovich had an assignment today: capture Jane Smith. He will have the same assignment tomorrow. And he knows where your group travels."

"He does? You do?" I asked.

"Yes." Reaching into his pocket, Deuxième pulled out another needle and vial.

I yelped and backed away. Deuxième chortled like a small boy.

"Not for Jane. This one," here he touched the needle, "This one is for Ivanovich. Tomorrow morning, before Deuxième rests, he will have boarded a train heading far to the east and he will inject himself with this medicine." His eyes twinkled with amusement. "Ivanovich will sleep all the day tomorrow. To Germany and beyond. Deuxième is making certain that Ivanovich does not do his day's work tomorrow. Or the next day." He laughed again.

"Why are you telling me this?" I asked. "Won't you get in trouble?"

Deuxième's voice dropped to a mere whisper. "Jane Smith saved Deuxième's life. Deuxième does not understand why, but he is grateful. Deuxième is thanking Jane today. *Merci*," he said, dropping his head in a slight bow.

"*De rien*," I said. "It was nothing." My cheeks burned. I'd almost killed him and he wanted to thank me for saving him.

He smiled sadly. "It was a great deal more than nothing. Deuxième understands about indebtedness."

As I tried to think of a way to apologize for bringing a roof down on his head, the air rippled and he disappeared.

Will ran towards me, Mickie just behind him.

"Sam!" she cried, throwing her arms around me. "Are you alright?"

"Yeah," I said. "I'm . . . fine." *And mildly shocked by the turn of events*, I thought to myself.

"What did he say when he spoke in French?" asked Mickie.

"We couldn't hear him," said Will.

I still didn't want to admit in front of Mickie that I'd saved the life of someone who worked for Helga. "Uh," I said, "He wanted to warn me that Helga is on my trail."

"*Warn* you?" said Will.

"Why would he warn you?" asked Mickie. "I thought he worked for her."

"He does," I said. Inside my shoes, my toes curled and uncurled. "But I guess he doesn't see eye to eye with her about everything."

"*He* doesn't? Or Ivanovich doesn't? Or both of them don't?" asked Will.

I frowned. "I think it's just him. Deuxième. I think Ivanovich would hand me over in a heartbeat."

"The whole thing makes no sense," said Mickie. "From now on, we stick together. Sir Walter, too. No more chasing voices in his head."

"That's not reasonable," began Will.

"Reasonable?" asked Mickie, her voice shrill in the dark night. "*Reasonable*? What is reasonable about a thug rippling right in front of me and putting me in a fireman's hoist? It could have been the other one. The Russian-guy."

From what I could gather, Mickie had missed the fact that she'd also been drugged. Maybe it was better that she didn't know, all things considered.

I wrapped an arm around Mickie's shoulder. "It's okay," I said. "He's gone. He only wanted to help."

"Any sign of Sir Walter?" demanded Mickie.

The French gentleman rippled solid beside us. "I am difficult to see when I wish to avoid being seen." Smiling, he turned to me. "*Mademoiselle* Sam, you handled that with great confidence and good judgment."

"I'll say," agreed Will.

I felt a small happy fluttering in my stomach.

"We could have used you back there," said Mickie to Sir Walter.

"If you had, indeed, been in need of me, I would have materialized sooner," he replied. "Ivanovich and Deuxième have, the both of them, a quite healthy fear of me. Had I appeared, I think Deuxième might have transported you involuntarily. And, as I pointed out a moment earlier, *Samanthe* had things well in hand without my interference."

"She kept her cool, alright," said Will. He mussed his sister's hair, murmuring to her, "Unlike some I could mention."

"Ouch!" said Mickie. "Hands off the hair. My head is killing me."

I fingered the vial in my pocket. "Yeah, um, Deuxième said that might be a side effect."

"Of what?" asked Mickie and Will at the same time.

"Uh, well, he kind of . . . drugged you," I said to Mickie. "To keep me from running away without hearing him out."

"Oh," said Mickie, frowning. "I don't remember that part."

"Yeah," I said. "He's really fast with needles. You were out before I even caught up to you. He gave me something to take the pain away." I held up the small vial of clear liquid.

Mickie grimaced. "I don't think so."

Sir Walter chuckled beside Will. "If it is of his own making, it will do exactly what he said it would do. And exceptionally well, I might add."

"I'll stick with a Coke and some Advil," said Mickie.

"Let's get out of here," said Will. "Before Deuxième changes his mind."

I looked one last time down the dark alley, shuddering.

21

COLD AS ICE

Our group spent the Sunday before Christmas traveling to Annecy, the "Venice of France," where we had a chance to breathe the chill air of mountains bordering Switzerland. Mickie kept a close eye on me, with all the water surrounding us, but I stayed solid, even when Will and I ran beside the lake, its dark waters haunting and pristine.

There were no organized French Club activities the second day, and since the snow had accumulated during the night, we stayed indoors. Sir Walter planned to begin training Will and myself in self-defense for chameleons. We had plenty of room in yet another extravagant two-bedroom suite, which Sir Walter confessed to having arranged, both this time and in Paris.

"I think," said Sir Walter, "We should begin with a basic rescue technique. There are certain circumstances under which even chameleons find it difficult or impossible to ripple and thus might require assistance."

"That happens for me a lot," I said, frowning.

"Ah, yes," said Sir Walter. He smoothed his goatee thoughtfully. "And yet, you had the *ability* to ripple from a young age, did you not?"

"It happened once, for sure, just after I lost Mom," I agreed.

"But she didn't get in years of practice, like Will," said Mickie.

"That will have made the difference," said Sir Walter. "It is unlikely, *Samanthe,* you will ever have the facility that your friend Will enjoys."

"Thanks for the vote of confidence," I muttered.

Sir Walter chuckled. "Forgive me. Your own abilities may develop significantly. However, Will *ree-pills* like no one I have ever before seen."

"Will had trouble rippling once," said Mickie, her brows drawn tightly together.

"I did?" asked her brother.

"You were five," she began, "Dad rang the doorbell and you were all excited to see him. I told you not to open the door, but you did anyway, and he clocked you before you could get away."

"Yeah, I remember that," said Will. "Mick was shouting at me to ripple away after Dad hit me, only I

205

was like, I don't know, too tired or something. I just couldn't make myself disappear."

My stomach clenched. It was wrong that a five-year-old wasn't safe opening the door to see his dad.

Sir Walter spoke. "If a chameleon retains less than complete consciousness, rippling becomes nearly impossible."

"Well, for sure my head spun in circles when Dad hit me," said Will.

"Your face looked so white," Mickie murmured, the memory still raw.

"Loss of blood, being nearly asleep, over-exertion: any of these can make rippling difficult," said Sir Walter. "I carried smelling salts for many years in case I should need to revive myself. Perhaps we would all be wise to do so once again."

"But back to Sam," said Will. "She can get better if she keeps practicing?"

"Of course," said Sir Walter. "In fact, I think we should allow Sam the first opportunity to attempt the rescue technique of which I spoke." He turned and smiled at me. "*Mademoiselle,* having already been a victim of this technique, I believe you understand the principles."

I stared at him blankly.

"When Deuxième stole away with you, yes?" said Sir Walter.

"Oh," I said. "You want me to try taking someone with me when I ripple?"

He executed a tiny bow. "If you would be so good as to take hold of *Mademoiselle* Mackenzie and ripple away?"

"No, no, no," said Mickie, holding her hands up as she backed away. "This body is off limits, thanks very much."

Sir Walter raised one eyebrow and Will turned away, chortling.

"There may come a time when it would be well for *Samanthe* to ripple away with you," said the French gentleman.

Will rolled his eyes. "C'mon, Mick, that was years ago."

"Not going to happen," she said, crossing her arms.

Will groaned. "It was only bad 'cause you had the stomach flu."

"Yeah, well I didn't think much of your cure," Mick grumbled.

"One time I grabbed her out of the kitchen when she was about to puke all over the table," said Will.

"He didn't bother to mention that bodily functions would resume as soon as we came solid again," said Mick, thwacking his arm with a pillow.

"I didn't know," Will admitted. He was trying hard not to grin.

"Mickie," I said, attempting to not sound demanding, "I'd really like the chance to try this while there's no lives hanging in the balance."

She turned her head to one side, sighing heavily. I thought I could bring her around.

I spoke again. "I don't know if I'd be here today if your brother hadn't rescued me using this technique."

One of Will's hands flew to his forehead. His sister looked over at him, first curious, then suspicious.

"Will?" Mickie's voice came out in a low growl. "Is there something you'd like to tell me?"

Will scuffed at the carpet. "No."

Suddenly I remembered that Mickie didn't know about the trip Will and I had taken to Helga's lab. That she wasn't supposed to know. Ever. "Oh, crap," I mumbled.

"Will?" Mick's voice raised a few decibels.

She was working up a full head of steam. This wasn't going to be pretty. I hoped maybe I could deflect some of her anger from her brother.

"It was my fault. I talked Will into going back to Dr. Gottlieb's lab," I said. "I knew she had all these other black books like the one we got from Pfeffer, and I wanted to get them."

"You—*you what*?" Mickie stood, as angry as I'd ever seen her. "Will? You went *back* to UC Merced?" She ground fists against her hips, elbows flaring.

Will crossed his arms. "Yeah, so deal with it already."

"Deal with it? *Deal with it?*" Her voice rose in an awful crescendo. "*What were you thinking about?* I can't believe this!" She turned to me, her face blotched red with anger. "And you—how could you do this to us?"

I felt my face warming.

"These people are *killers*, Sam," said Mickie.

"She *knows* that, Mick." Will's low voice cut across her frantic one.

"But she obviously doesn't *get* it, does she?" Mickie shot back at her brother. "They *killed* Professor Pfeffer!"

My throat shrunk tight.

"That's *enough*, Mick. She gets it."

Mickie ignored the angry edge in her brother's voice. "Do you think they'd hesitate to do the same to you, or to me and my brother?"

"*I said enough, Mick!*" Will spoke with authority as he locked eyes with his sister.

Finally I found my voice. "You're not the *only* person in the room who lost someone to those murderers," I said, my voice shaking.

Mickie made an angry, exasperated noise and rose. She headed for the hotel suite door, kicked over a small side table in her way, and slammed the door behind her so hard that the pictures on the wall rattled.

209

I looked at Will. His face was turned from me in profile. Without even blinking, he stared at the carpet. He avoided looking at me. I saw the tension in his hands, balled into fists, and in the throbbing vein at his temple. "I'll work on damage control." He didn't sound angry; he sounded cold as ice and a million miles away from me.

22

SHAM-SUNDAR

Without once looking at me, Will exhaled noisily and exited the room following his sister.

Tears rushed to fill my eyes. For several minutes Sir Walter and I sat in the room without speaking. When he stood, I assumed he planned to leave me as well, but he surprised me by returning with a box of tissues. He handed them to me without a word, and I began drying my face.

At last Sir Walter spoke. "I do not pretend to understand your motivation, nor will I insist that you explain yourself to me now. What is done is done."

I sobbed, wondering how badly I'd damaged my friendship with Will. His earlier warnings rattled around inside my head: *My sister can never know about this, okay?*

"However," continued Sir Walter, "I am less inclined to see this as the dangerous step that *Mademoiselle* Baker believes it to be. You are all alive, and what is more, unlikely ever to return so close to Helga's lair."

I stared at him. "What do you mean, unlikely to return so close?"

"Of course you cannot return to your home," he said.

"I have to go home."

He raised an eyebrow and looked at me, puzzled.

"I'm not leaving my family," I said. "It would kill Dad to lose me." As I spoke the words aloud, I realized the awful choice before me. I might not be able to leave Las Abs, but Will would almost certainly not return. The thought of a future without him left a hollow feeling where my stomach should be.

"Well, we have several days remaining to us during which we can discuss what would be best," said Sir Walter.

"There's something else," I said. I felt a cold determination building inside of me. I was done with keeping secrets. "I have good reason to believe that Deuxième survived the collapsed chamber because of me."

"Indeed?" Sir Walter looked surprised.

I explained how I'd called for assistance, adding that Deuxième held himself in my debt.

"This is most interesting. Most interesting, indeed." He tugged at his tiny beard a few times and sighed. "And now, if you will excuse me, my dear, I should like to *ree-pill*. I find I do my best thinking when my flesh makes no demands upon me."

"Of course," I said.

He stepped over and gently placed a hand upon my shoulder. "All will be well," he said. "We know Helga's wishes more clearly because Deuxième believed himself to be in your debt. All will be well." He smiled, patted my shoulder, and vanished.

I shut myself in my room and lay upon the narrow bed. After kicking my shoes off, I curled into a tight ball. Outside the sky remained a flat grey that couldn't clear and wouldn't snow. I felt cold and dull within. When I thought of the chill in Will's voice as he left, I ached as though we'd already parted forever.

Soon, very soon, I would have to give up the one person in my life I couldn't live without. That was the future I saw now.

But how do you do that?

The sun set early; street-lamps glowed outside my window, and still I didn't move.

How could I give up the person that provided my life with meaning? How would I survive such a sacrifice day after day once I'd made it? The sky, heavy with cloud-cover, threw down the reflected lights of Annecy so that my room remained in a pewter-colored gloom. I did not rise to draw the curtains. Upon my bed, I coiled fetus-like and cried until my eyes were dry.

When the tears came no more, I felt a heavy quiet settle upon me. Turning my head to the window, I saw the starless sky, and in the lamp-light, snow falling in clumped flakes. *Christmas Eve comes tomorrow*, I thought.

Quietly, I rose and gazed out the window at a softened world. The snow had begun mounding over benches, bushes, and parked bicycles, resolving sharp angles into rounded forms. A snowfall like this would shut down school back in Las Abuelitas. I wondered how the people of Annecy would manage tomorrow's whitened world.

Sir Walter's words in Disneyland floated back to me as if upon the drifting snow: *I find myself able to act . . . for those who do live, but who will not know a tomorrow if I stand by and do nothing.* I sighed, letting the words settle deep within me. Feeling sorry for myself, feeling angry at Mickie or wounded by Will's cold gaze: these were luxuries I could not afford.

This is how you move on, I said to myself. *You move on when your heart has broken because moving on is the right thing to do.*

I didn't feel like turning my ten-euro dinner allowance into a trip outside for a meal, so I rummaged through my bag for snacks. Inside, I found butter cookies and a bar of chocolate. When I'd eaten them, I curled up on my bed and fell into a deep sleep.

Much later, I awakened to the sound of Will and Mickie returning to our rooms. One of them knocked gently. I sat up, rose, and opened the door. It was Will.

"You all right?" he whispered.

As I heard the kindness in his voice, I knew I was. Our small fracas earlier? That, I could survive.

"Mick and I," he gestured over his shoulder to his silent sister, "we just want to apologize for how we responded."

"Doesn't matter," I said. Because I knew what really, truly mattered to me now: doing the right thing and keeping Will safe.

"Come inside," I said, beckoning to Mickie as well. "There's more I need to tell you."

I explained how I'd saved Deuxième's life, adding Sir Walter's point that we knew Helga's plans better because of what I'd done.

Will stood silent, gazing at the snow-covered world outside my window. Finally he spoke. "That impulse you had, to save life instead of destroying it, that's a good thing, Sam."

"A tiny bit of beautiful in all this dark mess," said Mickie, stepping over to squeeze my hand.

In the shadows, I saw Will's smile.

"*Sham-sundar*," he said, uttering the Indian word.

"Sham-whozit?" asked Mickie.

"*Sham-sundar*. It means the beautiful and the dark together," said Will.

"Like this," I added, gesturing to the wintry night scene beyond the window. As we looked upon the silent beauty, flakes began drifting downward.

"*Sham-sundar*," murmured Mickie.

***

When it was time to split into smaller groups for our home-stay visits, Sir Walter encouraged us with the fact that Helga wasn't likely to know where we were traveling as he hadn't discussed it with our teacher, other than to say he'd be hosting us for Christmas. He took it upon himself to purchase First-Class tickets via bullet train. There were definite advantages to traveling with our wealthy friend, not the least of which was we didn't get lost during our train transfer.

I slept the final leg of the journey, waking only as we pulled into the station at Carcassonne. Sir Walter arranged a taxi and Will, Mickie, and I squashed into the back seat for the short drive in the dark. I could see nothing, but it was plain enough we drove on a narrow and twisting road. We pulled into a gravel drive beside a small dwelling and tumbled out into the cool night air.

I set my bags down in the Barbie-sized bedroom Sir Walter indicated for me, six thousand miles from family and hugs on Christmas Eve. But I was not alone. In the front room, my three companions laughed heartily. A smile grew on my face. My chest feeling lighter, I shut my door, kicked off my boots, and clothes-still-on, crawled shivering into a bed that was soft and warm.

23

THE WELL OF JUNO

"*Joyeux Noël! Levez-vous, tout-le-monde!* Rise, rise, Happy Christmas!" The deep voice of Sir Walter roused me from dreams of hiking in Yosemite, the sun baking my neck. I kicked back covers that now stifled me. The house had warmed considerably since our late-night arrival.

It was Christmas morning. I smiled.

My skin felt scratchy from sleeping in my clothes, so I threw on clean ones and stumbled out into the main living area.

An inferno blazed in the stone fireplace and above the fire, threatening to drop into it, hung a pair of identical white tube-socks, drooping with odd-shaped items. Stockings? On Christmas morning in *France*?

I'd beaten Will out of bed, but Mickie was sitting with Sir Walter, drinking coffee and eating croissants. I crept toward the stockings and saw my name, written in Sharpie beside the other sock bearing Will's name. I grabbed mine and flopped at the table.

"Where's yours?" I asked Mickie, who was sneezing.

"I don't think *Père Noël* leaves them for adults," she said, blowing her nose.

"*Père Noël* puts treats in *shoes*," I said.

"Yeah, I already got that lecture from the resident expert in all things French." Mickie sniffled and stirred her coffee glumly.

"You got a cold?"

Mickie sneezed.

"Wow," I said. "Merry Christmas to you, huh?"

Mickie sneezed again.

"*Joyeux Noël!*" Sir Walter's eyes twinkled as he poured a cup of hot chocolate for me, thick as creek-mud.

"*Joyeux Noël,*" I replied. The cup radiated heat like a tiny midwinter sun in my hands.

"So open it, already," Mickie said, rattling my stocking upon the table.

I shook it empty. The tube-sock had been stuffed with American candy and French bons-bons and an envelope containing two crisp hundred-euro notes.

"Those are *not* from me, er, *Père Noël,*" Mickie said, tapping the bills. "Sylvia and your dad made me bring those, and I've been scared silly I'd lose them." She coughed into her elbow.

I read a card that must have held the money before I dumped everything out.

"I'm supposed to find something wonderful in France for Christmas," I said.

Will strolled into the room and mussed his sister's hair. "I'm wonderful. I'm in France."

I almost choked on my hot chocolate. Will looked like an ad for bed-head. I swallowed back desire and shifted my eyes away from *all I wanted for Christmas.*

His eyes darted to the fireplace. "Yes!" He grabbed his stocking, dislodged the contents onto a rug in front of the blaze, and began chugging the 330ml can of Dr. Pepper, ignoring the Skittles, Starbursts, Suchards and new toothbrush for the moment.

Then he smiled widely and ripped a phenomenal burp while saying "Merry Christmas" at the same time.

My angst-y feelings scurried and I burst into a fit of giggles.

Mickie said, "Bro, that was deeply disturbing," and sneezed.

Sir Walter politely ignored the performance.

"Are you sick, Mickie?" asked Will.

"Sick of you," she said, throwing a small package at him.

He caught and unwrapped the gift—a cell phone—and went over to his sister to give her a hug.

"Hello!" she said, pushing him away. "Major germs here."

"Thanks, Mick."

"Yeah, well, don't fall all over yourself about it. Stupid phone doesn't work in France, only in America."

As we sat around the table, Sir Walter explained his plans for the day.

"Tomorrow evening you travel to rejoin your group. Before that, I wish to take you to an important historical site of the region—"

Will grinned. "Sweet."

Sir Walter smiled and continued, "And then we will return in time for the midnight mass in the old city, followed by *la Reveille*."

I'd heard of *la Reveille,* the tradition of eating a huge feast after Christmas mass. Mickie looked confused, so I explained it to her.

"The midnight buffet sounds great," she said. "But I think I've seen enough historically significant things to last me several lifetimes. No offense, Sir Walter, but I'd actually prefer to spend the day nursing my cold by the fire. And maybe I'll give your translation of the black book another read-through."

Will crossed to hand his sister a fresh box of tissue and give her a hug. Mickie shoved him away. "Out of my air-space! Go breathe on something . . . historical."

After we'd finished breakfast, Will and I piled in a tiny Citroën car that our host had conjured out of an ancient garage.

"Not the front seat," warned Sir Walter.

Upon inspection, it appeared there was no front passenger seat to speak of. The springs were clearly visible through threads that had once been cloth. Clearly, this had been appropriated for other uses.

"Mice," said our French friend. "I need to keep a cat, but . . ."

He didn't finish the thought as he tried to start the engine a third time. Exiting the vehicle, Sir Walter lifted the hood and fumbled with the engine, crooning to it. He finished, chuckling.

"And no doubt you are thirsty, poor girl!" He opened the gas flap on my side and poured out the contents of a nearby gas can, sloshing a large portion down the side of the car. "Now we can be sure she will make the return trip!"

This time the car started.

"Are you sure this place will be open today? Everything's closed in America on Christmas Day," I said as we bounced along a tiny road, the hill-top village of Carcassonne receding behind us.

"It is less a matter of the site being open, and more a matter of knowing how to gain entrance," replied Sir Walter.

"More breaking and entering," I muttered to Will. "Terrific." My flat tone told him I thought it anything but terrific.

Will, however, just grinned.

"What do you know of the presence of ancient Rome in Gaul?" asked Sir Walter.

Will answered. "Not something we study much in America, but if I remember, it seems like Julius Caesar kicked your ancestors' butts, right?"

Sir Walter grunted, probably in assent. "The ancient Romans came to this region prior to Caesar in order to visit the hot springs. I am taking you to a place they considered quite holy, sacred to Juno. It was believed to be a propitious place for conceiving children—children marked by the blessing of the goddess."

The Citroën lurched as we turned onto a dirt road full of potholes. The poor car rattled as if bits and pieces would soon fall off, a bread-crumb-trail to help us back home. Sir Walter had to stop the car to open a gate that ran across the road.

"These lands were held by my family for seven hundred years," Sir Walter said.

"As in, this is yours?" Will asked, clearly impressed.

Sir Walter shrugged. "The present government of France does not think so. The land has been redistributed innumerable times in the past two centuries since *La Révolution*. I am not certain who is considered the present owner."

"Do you still think of this as your . . . home?" Will asked.

"Home." Sir Walter laughed softly to himself.

"Where you live, you know. Do you live here now?" Will asked again.

"My dear boy, I live a great many places now. But I retain no dwelling on a permanent basis. I have no need for it. A dwelling, in my condition, would be superfluous."

"I counted out that you've been staying solid about two and a half hours per day, on average," Will said.

"Very good," said Sir Walter. "You are correct."

It hadn't occurred to me to do the math on how he'd lived so long. A single happy thought fluttered through my belly: Will and I, together through oncoming centuries. But the thought of Helmann's plans for a thousand-year *reich* quickly squelched the dreamy image.

"I find it more convenient to live in dwellings maintained by others," continued Sir Walter. "Chenonceau, where we first met, is a favorite of mine.

Although I also appreciate modern touches from time to time."

"You just go from place to place?" I asked.

"Quite," he replied.

"How often do you need to eat and sleep?" Will asked.

"As I now live, I require a good meal twice a week, and I prefer to sleep once every week or so, although it is possible to pass many hours in a state resembling rest whilst one is in chameleon form," he replied. "This, as I mentioned before, would account for our friend Deuxième's ability to do without sleep in the conventional sense."

"Bodyguards that don't require sleep," began Will, "No wonder she didn't follow her brother's orders to kill them. They'd be invaluable."

"Hans instructed her last October to kill the bodyguards who had seen me," I explained. "Ivanovich was one of them."

"I'll bet that's why Deuxième—I mean Ivanovich—was invisible the time we went to Helga's lab together," Will said. "She's keeping her breeding experiments secret from Hans."

Sir Walter nodded. "She most certainly would not wish word to drift to her father that she is creating her own chameleons."

As we rounded a bend, Sir Walter struck a particularly deep pothole. The glove box popped unlatched, and a yellowed first aid kit fell onto the floor, open. Sir Walter ignored the disemboweling of the small compartment and parked, announcing we had arrived.

"There's not much here," said Will.

All I saw was a tumbled-down ruin. No telling what it had once been. A shrubby brush I didn't recognize covered the sloping hillside opposite the crumbled building. The sun shone weakly on the empty landscape, and I heard wind whispering through the shrubs. Sir Walter bent forward and tore a small fist-full of dirt from the cold ground. Bringing the earth to his nose, he inhaled as though scenting a fine wine. Then he stood and surveyed the ruin.

"This castle stood proudly once," whispered our ancient friend.

He directed our gaze to the collection of stones piled atop one another. A wall remained, perhaps ten feet high in places. Most notably, just beside us, stood a circular staircase within what must once have been a mighty tower. No entrance was visible however, either to the tower or through the wall.

"That's an arrow-slit!" shouted Will. "For firing on your enemies. It's narrow so they can't get a shot back at you."

Sir Walter chuckled. "A good marksman can send an arrow through that abbreviated window."

Will looked at Sir Walter with doubt. "That would be some shot."

"More easily accomplished as a training exercise than in the actual conditions of battle," admitted Sir Walter.

"Let's explore!" said Will, his eyes wide with glee.

"Unfortunately, the ruin is unsafe to explore. Too many stones have been borrowed for other uses through the years," said the old gentleman.

Kind of like your front passenger seat, I thought.

"Any part of the castle could disintegrate, and how would I explain such injuries to your sister?" asked Sir Walter.

"We could ripple," said Will, eyeing the structure wistfully.

"Perhaps," said Sir Walter. "But I bring you today to discover what lies beneath. Since we are without Mackenzie, we will pass invisibly through the earth to our destination below-ground."

"I'm game." Will looked at me. "If Sam is, I mean."

"*Pour-quoi-pas?*" I said. *Why not?*

"*Excellent,*" said Sir Walter, speaking the word with its pronunciation in French. "It has been many years since I taught chameleons such as yourselves, but there are skills and defenses it would be well for you to know, and passing together underground will give us the means to exercise one of those skills. I had meant

227

to teach you the other day, in Annecy, but . . ." He broke off, too much of a gentleman to mention how my confession had interrupted the lessons he'd planned for us that day.

He continued. "Are you well-versed in the *communication silent?*"

"Silent communication?" Will changed the word order from French to English.

"This is the method to communicate when you have both *ree-pilled*," he said.

"You mean how we can pass images to and from each other's minds?" I asked.

"You, my dear, may have an ability to do more," mused Sir Walter. "But more of that later. For now, I shall tell you a tale as we pass into the side of the mount. A *silent* tale. Gather hands, and do not let go until I indicate to you that it is time to solidify."

We held hands, Will's warm in mine. The feeling turned my stomach to pudding. This was all I needed to ripple, and I felt Will disappear at the same moment I did.

"Well done, Mademoiselle Samanthe."

Sir Walter's voice spoke—within in my mind. This was something Will and I had never experienced when sharing memories or images. *How did he do that,* I wondered.

"*With practice, my dear*," came his response. "*Do not allow yourselves to melt into anything else prior to re-materializing.*"

I saw Will's response: he replayed images of the moment I'd rematerialized with my pony-tail stuck in Bridget's rock wall. It looked pretty scary seen from Will's point of view, and a shudder ran through whatever *me* existed at the moment.

"*That is precisely what we wish to avoid*," said Sir Walter. "*Check always twice before solidifying. And now,* allons. *Straight ahead, maintaining always the hands together.*"

Invisible, we carved a silent passage through brush, soil, and rock, and after a half-minute, we broke through to a cavern pierced several times overhead with shafts of light. The floor of the castle above had evidently crumbled in places, creating the openings for daylight. The dark hollow was perhaps forty feet across. As my vision adjusted, I saw a pool of clear water, steaming, with a large irregular stone at its center. The top of the rock broke through the surface, and light from one of the shafts focused the current hour's sunlight upon the stone. The surrounding water gleamed and threw reflective ripples upon the cavern roof.

Stunning. It would've made me catch my breath if I'd had actual lungs.

The scene before me seemed to shift, and I realized Sir Walter was sharing a memory; it was as if he'd turned on a video. In his mind's eye, candles illuminated the cavern. No light spilled from the ceiling; this memory was from a time before the castle had tumbled to ruins. A woman with three small children dressed like Renaissance Fair re-enactors approached the water's edge. The woman spoke to them in what resembled French, which I could *hear* clearly. Her accent was strange as were many of her words. She spoke to the children of power and refuge; the girl and one boy listened with rapt attention. A second boy scowled and looked away. I heard Sir Walter like a voice-over in my head, commenting upon the scene he shared from his past.

She tells the enfants, the children, that this place is the source of their abilities. She tells them to keep their knowledge of this place secret—that it is their refuge should soldiers come to kill them. She shows them stores of food and wine, weapons and candles, and tells them the water is good for thirst but must not be soiled.

I found my eyes could shift focus from the room in-the-present to the room as-it-was in Sir Walter's memory, making strange ghostly shapes of the solid children and the woman at the well. The image shimmered, faded entirely, and we stood alone once more, hands within immaterial hands.

Sir Walter solidified, loosing Will's hand. Will rippled next and, sliding my hand from his, I followed.

"What *was* that?" Will asked, voice echoing softly in the womb-like space.

"I allowed you to see into the past, into my own childhood, so that you would see what my five-year-old self saw."

"And the woman?" Will asked.

"My mother," Sir Walter replied. "Foster-aunt to my cousin *Elisabeth* and aunt to young *Girard*, before he became known as *L'Inferne.*"

"Oh. The grim-faced boy," I said softly. Strange to think that Helmann had ever *been* a child himself.

"Is this the place you spoke of, the place the Romans revered?" asked Will.

"The Well of Juno," replied Sir Walter. "Yes."

I gazed at the steam rising off the water. "A hot-springs," I said. "We have them where I was born."

"Yes, I rather imagined you must," said Sir Walter, his voice a bare whisper.

I flushed, hoping he wouldn't ask me to elaborate, and walked towards the pool, noticing steps carved from the living rock, leading down into the water. "There's pyrite in the rock," I said, catching the shimmer of fool's gold.

"Indeed," said Sir Walter. "And true gold: auriferous pyrite, arsenopyrite, iron ore. The ancient Romans, and indeed my own family, lacked the technology to remove the gold. The Romans prized the iron ore in the area which led them to finding this spring and others. The spring was not underground in Roman times. My ancestors, the ones whose *derrières* the Romans did not kick—" Sir Walter paused here to wink at Will. "My family built a chamber and later the castle to guard the well."

"Did the Romans name all the springs in this area for different gods?" Will asked.

Sir Walter's lips curved into a half-smile. "No, indeed. Only very auspicious places were so named. My ancestors learned old tales that had survived over a millennia, Roman tales that reveal the origin of this unusual combination of the earth and the heavens.

"The story my mother recounted to me was of a great fiery missile from heaven. It landed upon what was then a marsh. The Roman soldiers who watched its descent reported it to their priests. The priests divined that this form," Sir Walter said, pointing to the stony mass in the pool, "Was a representation of Juno, who had chosen this location for a place of worship. At this time Juno caused the spring to form, and from those days three-hundred years before the birth of our Lord until the time my six-times great-grandfather won the lands twelve centuries later, it was a sacred place.

"In my mother's day, the place was consecrated to the Holy Virgin Mary and known only to the most trusted members of our family."

"So, that's a meteor," said Will, pointing at the form in the water.

Sir Walter nodded. "Containing tobiasite and other less rare elements."

"Yeah," said Will. His face flushed and mine followed suit knowing what Sir Walter might bring up next.

The French gentleman looked at us. "Your sister also understands the curious effect these elements have upon the developing fetus?"

"Well, just what you said in the letter," Will replied.

"The reason my family kept this spring a secret—indeed, the reason Romans regarded this as an auspicious place to . . . procreate—to start a child, yes?"

We nodded, eager to move to the next subject.

"It is the water—the water is contaminated by the heavenly element and the presence of gold within the bedrock. The map, yes? The dots correspond closely to sites where gold and tobiasite are found together in a heated spring. A woman who conceives here, this woman will give birth to one who carries the genetic code for Helmann's disease."

Curious, I asked, "And the following generations? Will they have Helmann's?"

"In some cases it appears, in other cases it is suppressed," replied Sir Walter.

"Like the genetic marker for breast cancer," Will said.

"Quite so." Sir Walter looked at Will, his eyes troubled. "Have you or your sister had genetic testing performed upon you?"

I made a small snorting noise. "No way would Mick let that happen."

"That is well. Girard controls two of the agencies that perform such testing in your country. I suspect he obtains information from laboratories outside his control as well, as a means of identifying any carriers of the chameleon gene."

"So this is where it all started," I said stirring the water with one hand. It was warm, inviting on such a cold day.

"This is one place among several," said Sir Walter. "You now know a good deal more than is safe to repeat. Perhaps this morning we might focus on safety—upon ways to defend yourselves and to protect those you hold dear."

"That's what I'm talking about," said Will.

I nodded. I wanted to know how to protect my family.

Just then, the peace of our small cavern was disturbed by a loud noise, like a door being opened. A door heavy enough to send echoes through the walls. I watched as small ripples ran across the pool.

"*Merdre!*" Sir Walter's cursing didn't sound good. "How did I miss their thoughts?"

We heard the sound of feet approaching.

"I behaved like a fool bringing you here without first coming alone. We are in grave danger. We must disappear at once." Sir Walter reached for one of my hands and Will took the other. "Keep hold!"

I felt their icy touch as they disappeared. The sound of several feet came closer. I tried. I really tried. But I couldn't ripple.

Will's cold invisible hand pulled out of mine and he solidified beside me. "You can do this Sam, I know you can!"

I pictured the creek in Yosemite. Imagined Will's arms around me. None of it helped. My heart raced and my mind refused to calm.

"What is it?" asked Sir Walter, solidifying beside us.

"She's having trouble rippling." Will looked worried.

Sir Walter turned his head towards stairs from which the sounds came. "Will, you must go now. Return to the car and await our arrival."

"I'm not leaving Sam."

"Go!" I whispered. "*Now*, you idiot!"

"I'm staying right here." His voice echoed, deep and firm, and my stomach squeezed.

Sir Walter cursed again. "Keep silent. Allow me to do the talking." He placed himself in front of us, protective, hands on hips. "Do not fear," he whispered to me. From the stairway across the cavern, two men entered holding guns.

24

DR. GOTTLIEB

The first man was compact, shorter even than Sir Walter, dark-haired and light-eyed. He held his weapon as an extension of himself, someone accustomed to carrying a gun. I'd never seen him. The second man, tall, had blond hair and glacier-blue eyes. I felt Will's grip tighten upon my hand: Ivanovich. We kept silent as Sir Walter had directed.

Sir Walter spoke first. "*Joyeuses Fêtes, Messieurs*," he said, wishing them happy holidays.

The two men grunted evil laughter. Ivanovich taunted Sir Walter with his pistol while the short man grabbed Will into an arm lock and held his gun to Will's head. I gasped, so afraid for Will that I barely noticed when Ivanovich did the same to me a second later.

"Let her go," said Will and Sir Walter at the same time.

I winced as Ivanovich tightened his grip.

Sir Walter's eyes darted from person to person, hatching who knew what plans.

"You've got me," Will said.

"They've pretty much got both of us," I pointed out, earning a sharp tug upon my twisted arm. I gasped in pain.

"The little girl is right," said Ivanovich as he struck Will on the jaw.

Will exhaled hard and fast, but didn't cry out.

"*Die Mutter* approaches," said Will's captor to Ivanovich. "Are you sure she'll want them alive?"

"Alive," said Ivanovich, grinning evilly. "For now."

I didn't know how I'd ever thought Deuxième resembled Ivanovich; the two appeared so different to me now.

We heard footsteps once more and turned our eyes to the staircase which had divulged the first two men. Looking small in the vastness of the cavern she entered, Helga Gottlieb, impeccably dressed in a dark grey suit, stepped into our view.

My breath quickened and my gut seized into a tight, hard lump. No way were we getting out of here alive.

"Cousin," she said, meeting Sir Walter's eyes. "How long it has been."

Sir Walter did not return her greeting.

Helga carried no weapon that I could see, but she didn't need to; she had henchmen for that.

"What a lovely Yuletide gift you have brought to me." Helga looked greedily at Will and myself.

Then she turned to address Sir Walter. "Their lives must mean a great deal to you that you remain here in plain view." She nodded curtly to the man holding Will. Swiftly, he fired a single shot at Sir Walter.

It felt to me as if the floor pitched sideways; my legs gave way. But Sir Walter had time to smile before rippling to safety. Just as quickly, he reappeared, the danger having been averted. Ivanovich jerked me upright and I snapped alert, my arm throbbing with pain.

"It was worth the attempt," said Helga, sighing.

"This one, now. . ." She eyed Will while addressing me. "A lover perhaps? Or a brother?" Her eyes grew wide at the tantalizing prospect.

"He's no one," I said, desperate to protect him.

"Hmm . . . but if I fire upon him, will he disappear or will he bleed?"

"Don't shoot him!" I called out. "I'm the one you want. Let him go."

She paused, considering her next move.

Ivanovich's grip upon my arm loosened and I hear him sigh lightly, as if in relief from something painful.

"Ivanovich," called Helga. "Is this the boy who stole into my laboratory?"

She knew! All our caution had been for nothing. Just like our theft of the worthless journal. Worse than nothing. Somehow, we'd shown our identities. Despair welled up inside me.

I flicked my eyes to look at Ivanovich's cold eyes. But their fire had gone out. Slowly, Helga's thug shook his head "*No*."

"You are certain?" Helga demanded.

Beside me, the creature she had tormented for untold years nodded a "yes."

And then I knew! I knew with complete certainty that it was no longer Ivanovich but Deuxième who held me.

Emboldened, I called to Helga. "Let the boy go. His blood holds no secrets," I said, glancing to Deuxieme. "Let the boy go and I'll serve you."

Her gaze, fierce and feral, fell upon me. "Oh, you will serve me," she said, her voice a deadly whisper. "Have no doubt upon that score." She turned to Will's captor.

"He dies," she said, indicating Will.

At the same moment the bullet left the chamber, Will vanished to safety and did not reappear.

Helga, caught by surprise, swore softly.

The hairs along my neck raised; her calm felt more deadly than her rage.

Beside me, Deuxième whispered, "Run! Take the stairs!"

I didn't need any encouragement, but he must have feared otherwise. He threw me towards the stairs, and my arms and legs wind-milled as I scrambled to cross the cavern without falling. From one corner of my vision, I saw Sir Walter ripple invisible and heard his voice, deep and resonant, within my mind. "*Go*," he said. "*Leave Helga and her creatures to me.*" I ran onwards.

Then I felt an icy cold wash through me. "Will?" His name escaped my lips as I clambered to the ancient stairs. It had to be Will! Helga was still shouting. Looking over my shoulder to be sure, I confirmed that Deuxième remained solid. But just before the cavern closed from view, I saw an awful sight. Helga raised a small pistol and aimed it at Deuxième.

He crumpled and at the same moment, Sir Walter rippled solid. I hesitated on the stairs. Sir Walter, evading Helga, grabbed the shorter man and rippled away with him. I turned back to the stairs, scrambling up the ancient, worn surface. I felt the icy blast again.

Go to the car! I hurled the words to Will from within my mind, adding a visual image of the same phrase. *Go to the car!* I couldn't let Helga get her hands on Will, and I had the advantage of being someone she wanted *alive*, not dead. *Go to the car! Wait for me there!*

Up the cavern stairs I ran, feeling power in my runner's legs—I was made for this! I burst into daylight and sprang across an ancient courtyard. A few broken paving stones remained scattered upon the uneven ground. Shrubs scratched my jeans as I dashed for a place to screen and calm myself. Walls cut me off from the ground and no rooms remained in which I could hide. The spiral staircase! Just another few feet. The treads on the staircase were deep and worn in the center. As I climbed, some of the steps had crumbled almost away. But suddenly, there I was, at the topmost step.

I crawled up into what had once been an arrow-slit in the tower. Now it was a gaping window large enough to shelter me from sight; you'd have to climb far within the spiral tower to notice me.

Our car waited below; I didn't see Will.

I hunkered down. Wind whistled past me, in and out of tiny chinks in the ancient stone tower. To one side, all was open air and a fall of several stories. I grabbed a solid-looking bit of wall on the precipice and held tight, trying to quiet my mind, hoping I wouldn't be followed, wouldn't be found. Shifting one foot for balance, I dislodged a rock. I cringed as it rolled lazily off the tower, bouncing noisily onto the graveled road beside our car.

Great.

"Come down!" Helga's voice, strong and authoritative, called to me from below.

I laughed. I couldn't help it. Her request was ridiculous. And laughing made me feel braver. *Seriously? She thinks I'd march down to her?* But then I stopped laughing, because there wasn't anything funny about being trapped at the top of a tower.

What was I thinking?

I looked through the broken window. Was there another way down? I had reasonable skills on the gym rock wall; could I climb down the outside of this tower?

Helga spoke again. "Come down to me and perhaps your father and step-mother will yet live in their drowsy little town. What is it called? Ah, yes. Las Abuelitas."

My heart froze. *She knows who I am. And how to hurt me.*

"Or we can do things more . . . painfully," she continued. "There are many ways to extend the life of the dying. I have made it something of a hobby of mine to learn what human flesh can endure."

I shrank at her words. "You're evil!" I whispered. Which only made me sound like a child. Something inside me stirred, shifted, and I felt a growing need to command her respect. If she was going to hunt me down like prey, I wouldn't be the mouse this time. I would be a lioness. Agile. Stealthy. Deadly.

She crept towards the base of the tower, speaking casually of the pains she would inflict upon Sylvia while my father watched.

But she wasn't the only one who could use words as weapons.

"Helmann won't like that," I called, my voice strong and clear.

"How dare you name my father!" she cried.

My barb stings, does it? I felt emboldened.

"He's already pissed at you," I added. "He kicked you out of Geneses, didn't he?"

"Silence, child!"

"Does he know about your little genetic experiment? Your son?"

Helga growled her hatred of me. Now I could hear her climbing the staircase. I looked around for something to throw. I would not go down without a fight this time. Beneath my right foot, a rock shifted. Angling my foot back and forth, I loosened the stone 'til I thought I could ease it free. As I grasped it, the rock dropped heavily on one of my left fingers. I inhaled sharply at the pain.

Breathing through the hurt, I hoisted the weapon with my uninjured hand. When I looked up to see how far Helga had come, she'd vanished. *Crap!* I thought. She'd rippled and could reappear anywhere. *No*, the cool logic flowing through me said. She couldn't come solid on either side of me—no room—nor could she ripple behind me. That meant she could only come solid in front of or below me. For a split second, I wondered if I might be able to ripple now that I'd tamed my fear. But no. I couldn't simultaneously prepare to bash Helga with a rock and relax into peaceful nothingness. I shifted my weight to gain additional stability. A few rocks at my feet tipped and settled. *This whole place is crumbling to pieces!*

Helga materialized not ten feet below me, holding a gun which she pointed at me.

"I'm no use to you dead," I said, hefting the stone in my right hand.

"Nor can you run away if I blow your kneecap off," she retorted.

"Do that and I'll lose my balance," I pointed out. "The drop will kill me."

She frowned; she'd already figured this out. The gun was a bluff.

I looked into the ice-blue eyes of the woman who had tormented poor Deuxième—who had probably left him for dead.

"If you come any closer, I'll jump," I said, resolve hardening as I spoke.

"Very well," she said, placing the revolver into a pocket. "So here is what will happen. Should you jump, I will vanish and travel to your charming home town."

I felt cold prickles in my stomach.

She climbed the stairs towards my nest, slowly, someone who knew she had no need to hurry.

"I'll count backwards from ten, shall I? And you decide what you would prefer. You can come with me voluntarily, or you can jump." She began her count. "Ten. Nine." She took another two steps closer to me. "Eight. Seven. You might just survive that fall, you know. Horribly maimed, of course."

I looked away from her terrible glacial eyes, mesmerizing as oncoming headlights.

"Six. Five. Certainly you'd be too injured to follow me to Las Abuelitas." She smiled and continued her inexorable progress. "Four. Three. But I don't think you'd enjoy watching what I have in mind." She hissed the last words.

I lifted the stone. My last defense.

Her mouth curved up on one side. "Really, child." Another step towards me.

My legs shook beneath me.

"Two. . . and one." She stood before me, only a few stairs between us. "What is it to be?"

I threw the stone, howling in anger at all she'd done, all she planned.

Helga rippled. The stone bounded harmlessly down the stairway. But I'd unbalanced myself as I threw the rock, and I lurched forward. As I fell, Helga's invisible form washed through me: cold, dark and evil. Tumbling head-over heels, I lodged hard against the curved wall of the staircase, the wind knocked out of me. Struggling to draw breath, I saw Helga ripple solid where I'd been a second before. She grabbed at the stone wall and kept herself from falling backwards. Roaring in anger, she turned, looking over her shoulder at me, hatred pouring from her eyes.

But as she turned, the gaping sill to which she clung gave way. Two, then six, then a dozen stones plummeted into the open air.

And so did Helga.

Wheezing, I crawled to the ragged new edge of the tower. Helga must have rippled as she fell; she was nowhere to be seen.

But as I searched the ground for her, I saw Sir Walter and Will rippling solid beside the car. Less than a second later, the air beside the old Citroën shimmered again. This time it was Helga. But she didn't pay close enough attention to her surroundings. Her left hand, thrown out behind her, materialized *within* the back of the car, at the gas-flap. There was a sound like several BB guns firing. Then I heard Helga yelping as she withdrew the bloodied hand that had solidified inside the car, displacing bits of metal. That explained the popping sounds.

Gas dripped lazily down the side of the Citroën as the three upon the ground below me regarded one another.

Glancing at her injured hand for only a second, Helga tucked it under her right arm. Then she aimed her gun at Sir Walter and fired. He rippled away and her bullet lodged in the walls of the ruin. The old gentleman came solid behind her and tried to grab her, but she rippled. He twisted round. Noticing me atop the tower, Sir Walter shouted to Will.

"Get Sam! Ripple with her!"

Will followed Sir Walter's gaze and met my eye. Just as the air around Will began to waver, Helga came solid and fired at him.

She missed, I thought. *She can't have hit him, dear God, please!*

I heard a small grunt from the stairs below me. Turning, I saw Will!

"You're alright," I said, taking the stairs two at a time to reach him, maybe ten steps below me.

Will grinned as he climbed the stairs towards me. But his hoodie, pale-gray, discolored as a blossom of red appeared below his left shoulder. Will seemed to stumble, and then his eyes rolled up, and he collapsed upon the ancient stairs.

"No," I cried, jumping down the remaining treads.

The fall had jolted him; he was conscious again when I reached him.

"Hey." He sounded winded, like he'd just run a hard race. "I don't feel so . . . just give me a minute."

"Take your time," I said, staring in horror at the patch of red, spreading slowly. I needed gauze; I needed bandages.

"Just another quick sec," said Will. "I'll grab you and we'll ripple together."

I thought of what Sir Walter had told us about times when rippling didn't work. Will's eyes fluttered; he remained conscious, but only just. I needed *sal volatile*—smelling salts!

I remembered the glove box tumbling open. "First aid kit!" I said aloud.

"Don't be ridiculous," mumbled Will, shifting to face me. As he turned, he saw the blood-red stain. "Oh," he sighed. "That explains a lot."

Below, Helga and Sir Walter traded insults like children at a playground. It seemed neither could defeat the other. But she had to escape him to get to me. Unfortunately, I knew that if she had to battle Sir Walter all day, she would.

A crazy idea came to me as I looked at Will, his eyelids drooping, his lips slightly parted, furrows deepening between his brows. Crazy, but genius. Something inside me wrenched open, flooding me with desperate courage. I was getting that first aid kit and getting us both out of here.

Crazy, said a voice inside as I brought my face over his 'til I could feel the flutter of breath as he exhaled. *Crazy,* repeated the voice. Will smelled like blood and

French detergent and pine needles. *Crazy.* I brought my mouth to his.

The sound of the two dueling below receded. I heard only a low sigh that came from inside one of us: I wasn't sure who. And Will's mouth tasted like the whisper of willows through my mind, and sunshine, and coming home. I thought he was kissing me back, and then I was sure of it.

His lips on mine felt like the slow embrace of rippling through glass.

My hands on his face trembled.

Then they didn't.

I'd rippled.

Without a backward glance at the boy I loved, I shot up the stairs and hovered over the gap in the tower. Then, I set my invisible foot upon the ledge and stepped out into thin air.

Only it wasn't. The air felt thick as maple syrup and moving through it was a lot like swimming, like Sir Walter had said.

While I toppled earth-ward, Sir Walter and Helga battled on, rippling and solidifying in a bizarre dance.

"She's gone by now," said Sir Walter. "You've lost, cousin Helga."

Helga's cold eyes blazed as she came solid, slamming her foot within the graveled road so that pebbles exploded in an arc towards Sir Walter, like spray from a water-skier. Rippling, he dodged, although

250

the look on his face showed the move had surprised him.

I slid invisibly towards the far side of the car. Hunching low at the front passenger door, I came solid. Through the window, I could see the first aid kit spilled open below the seat. Sure enough, a small vial of *sal volatile* nestled between a thermometer and package of gauze. I eased the car door open as silently as possible. Helga was now shouting in German at Sir Walter, who had disappeared for longer than usual. Then Helga fell silent, and all I heard was her breath, fast and angry, and the whisper of wind through the shrubs. I reached for the first aid kit, stopping myself from shutting the car door, which Helga would have heard. Leaving it ajar, I crept backwards, towards a tall patch of scrubby brush. With the warmth of Will's lips still upon my own, I knew rippling would come easily.

I reached the brush and eased myself behind. I'd made it!

Just before I closed my eyes to calm and ripple, a movement beside the car caught my eye. Straining my head around the shrub, I watched, horrified, as the car door began, slowly and unstoppably, to fall shut on its own.

No, no, no! I thought. Every muscle in my body tensed as I waited, hoping against hope that Helga would start shouting again and miss the sound. She didn't. The door slammed noisily shut. No one could have missed that.

Helga spun and fired at the source of the noise, the bullet's impact creating sparks and sudden flame. Some idiotic California-bred impulse to warn people about fire made me twitch from behind the brush that hid me.

Helga saw me, eyes ablaze with her lust to possess me. But I felt an inferno in my own belly. Today, I was the lioness. I had someone to protect, and Helga was not going to get in my way. I felt my lips pull back as she fired again, missing me. Yes, I was actually baring my teeth as I prepared to ripple away.

What happened next seemed impossible.

Out of nowhere, there came a thunderous noise like a cannon blast, and the Citroën, and Helga Gottlieb with it, exploded into an yellow ball of heat. The blast knocked me backwards, and I lay staring stupidly at a sky the color of a robin's egg.

In the movies, explosions happen in slow motion. This felt like it happened in fast-forward. One moment Helga stared into my eyes, craving victory. The next moment, she was gone, without even the chance to ripple, and I lay on my back without any clear memory of the moment I'd hit the ground.

I tipped my head in the direction of the waves of hot air rolling toward me. A mistake. The sky spun in dizzy circles, and I squeezed my eyes shut, breathing in the smoldering odor of gasoline and things that weren't meant to burn. I lay there a moment, aware that there was something *important* that I needed to do.

"Will!" His name caught in my throat.

25

REST IN PEACE

I sat up, my head still spinning, and took several slow, deep breaths holding my shirt over my nose and mouth. I had to get to Will.

Sir Walter rippled solid beside me upon the ground.

"*Merci, Seigneur,*" he whispered. *Thank God.* To me he said, "*Mon Dieu,* but you frightened me!"

"Here," I said, handing him the first-aid kit. "Will's been shot. He's faint and he can't ripple. I thought maybe—"

Sir Walter cut me off. "*Sal volatile!* Of course."

"I'll be there in a moment," I said. "Just go—make sure Will's okay."

Sir Walter was gone.

I felt steadier with each moment. Ignoring the fire, I calmed myself and felt my body slipping into nothingness. The dizziness passed immediately, and I dashed to the tower, scrambled up the side and through the tiny window. Sir Walter had already removed Will's shirt and was unwinding a measure of gauze while pressing a pad to the gunshot wound.

I came solid beside the two.

"Go to Deuxième," said Sir Walter, without looking up.

"Will!" I tried to speak, but my voice caught, the words jumbling, tangling.

"Go to Deuxième!" said Sir Walter as he began the bandaging. "Quickly!"

"What?" I asked, grasping Will's lifeless hand in mine.

"Go! Deuxième trusts you. Leave Will to my care."

"You're—I'm not—No!" I said. "I can't leave Will like this."

Will's eyes fluttered open.

"Samantha, Deuxième is dying!" said Sir Walter.

"What about Will?"

Sir Walter turned from Will and looked at me, his face grave. "Will's alive. Deuxième may not be; Go, child. None of us deserves to die alone."

My heart felt as if Sir Walter had plunged an icy dagger into its center, but I stood.

"Hurry!" he called. "Seek the scent of our earlier trail."

Sir Walter thought I'd have to tunnel through to the cavern.

"There's a faster way," I called as I crossed the courtyard heading for the stairs. And yet, as I raced to re-enter the cavern of the well, I found that I *could* smell a whisper of Will's warm pine-y scent and Sir Walter's cologne. The ghostly waftings led me as I took the stairs below ground.

Deuxième lay beside the pool. His face, sickly, turned to the water.

"*Si beau,*" he whispered. *So beautiful.*

"I'm here, Deuxième," I said, sinking to his side.

"It is well," he said, a tiny smile upon his white lips.

His face appeared gray to me now.

"How cold Deuxième feels," he said.

I wrenched off my jacket, thick and warm. "Here," I said. "This will help."

"Ah, Jane Smith." He said my name in a sigh. "Deuxième is tired. So tired."

"Rest, my friend," I whispered to him. As I tried to tuck my jacket under his body, I gasped at the amount of blood already soaked into his garments.

"Deuxième would like to be free, as Jane said he is not," whispered the dying man.

"You're free of her," I said. "She . . . she's dead now."

"Ah, freedom. *La Liberté*," he whispered. "It has a good feeling, does it not, Jane Smith?"

"Yes, Deuxième," I said. Twin tears dropped from my eyes, landed upon his face.

"Jane weeps," he said.

"Yes, Deuxième, Jane weeps." Gently, I wiped the side of his face.

"Do not weep, Jane Smith. Deuxième wishes to rest now. Speak to me of a resting place."

"A resting place?" I stammered, wondering what he wanted. And then a memory returned to me from last summer.

"There's a place in Yosemite," I began. "A place where every summer the snow melt chases down into a shallow valley to become Illilouette Creek. Beside the creek it is so peaceful your heart aches." I took Deuxième's hand. "And the creek bottom is lined with rocks of every color you can imagine. Golds and browns and tans, pinks and yellows and creams, all spotted with shining bits of black embedded in the granite millions of years ago.

"The water runs clear and pure, because it's from melted snow, and sometimes you don't think you're looking at water at all. It's like glass, that water, until a breeze comes singing down the valley, setting the trees alive with chatter." I laughed, knowing I sounded ridiculous, but this was what I had to offer. "I have no idea what the trees are saying, Deuxième. It sounds solemn and peaceful, though. And the same breeze that makes the trees murmur comes down to the creek and wrinkles the surface so that you remember it isn't glass at all." Pausing, I heard a different kind of breath rattle from Deuxième's lips, and I knew he was gone. The Well of Juno fell silent. I gazed at the fallen star in the pool beside his body.

Sitting with him in the silent chamber of the well, I wept. "Rest, Deuxième," I said at last. "Rest in peace."

I stood to leave, feeling a sudden surge of panic about Will.

I don't remember my race up the stairs, across the courtyard, and up the first few stairs in the tower. Will lay resting, his head pillowed upon Sir Walter's jacket.

Sir Walter looked up at me, his brows raised in a silent question.

"Deuxième is gone," I choked out the words. I couldn't form sounds to ask about Will.

The old gentleman closed his eyes, sighing, then turned back to his patient. "Will?"

Will's eyes, tired and strained, opened slowly.

"It is time," said Sir Walter.

Will turned to me and I felt my face flush. I could think only of our kiss when I looked at him, but it was impossible to look away.

Sir Walter waved the *sal volatile* below Will's nose, and Will's eyes brightened. He sat up, blinking in the sunlight.

"Ready when you are," Will said.

Sir Walter nodded and explained to me, "Your friend will feel much better in his chameleon form. You and I, meanwhile, must bury poor Deuxième. I have asked Will to remain in physical contact with you whilst he is invisible. When you and I have finished our task, we shall join him to return to *Mademoiselle* Mackenzie."

I felt my cheeks burning hotter with the mention of physical contact, but nodded that I understood: this would be the best way to be sure Will remained "with" us. Then I thought of something. "Uh, Sir Walter?"

"Yes, my child?"

"We'll need, like, a shovel or something, won't we?"

He smiled. "I have something else in mind. Come."

I stood to follow Sir Walter as Will rippled and disappeared. A moment later I felt the chill of Will's touch upon my shoulder. *A cold shoulder.* Was there some awful symbolism happening here? Would Will brush our friendship aside now that I'd crossed an unspoken line by kissing him?

He kissed you back! I tried to find comfort in the idea, but did kissing back count when you were only semi-conscious? I pushed the thoughts aside. I had a job to do.

Sir Walter, as he crossed the barren courtyard, looked around as if to snatch memories from his former home. What would it be like if I came back to my house in Las Abs six hundred years from now? The pool would still be there, maybe, as a big hole in the ground. I shuddered again and jogged to catch up to the old gentleman.

As we re-entered the chamber of the well and approached Deuxième's body, Sir Walter sighed long and low. How many deaths had he seen, I wondered? And yet this thousandth death, of a man half his enemy, could touch and grieve the old man. My heart filled with love for Sir Walter.

"My dear *Samanthe*," he began, "With your assistance, I propose that we ripple with Deuxième's body between us and place him within these walls for his final rest."

"So, we'd have to be, like, both holding him, right?" I asked. "But what if we don't ripple at the same time?" I didn't want to think it through too carefully in case it involved something messy.

"I shall time my shift to yours." He smiled and added, "I am rather fast, my dear."

Yeah. I'd seen that a few minutes ago.

We knelt on opposite sides of Deuxième's body. As I slipped my arms beneath the body, I kept thoughts of kissing Will from materializing. Will's wintry touch upon my shoulder meant he'd "see" what I thought. Instead, I let my eyes rest upon the water beyond Sir Walter. Wispy hints of steam rose off of the still pool.

So peaceful, I thought. A sigh escaped me, and then I felt my flesh fading. Across from me, Sir Walter followed. Deuxième rippled with us, an airy nothing.

"Arise," said Sir Walter, his voice clear and firm within my mind. *"We shall place him behind the Madonna."*

As I glanced up, I saw a faded mural upon the chamber wall opposite us. We drifted toward it and then plunged within the wall. I smelled the chalk-dry whisper of stone.

"Release him," commanded Sir Walter.

I let slip my hands. *Goodbye Deuxième,* I said in silence.

I heard Sir Walter murmur familiar phrases. *Latin,* I thought.

I saw a message scrawled in Will's handwriting: *He's chanting a Requiem Mass.*

I waited, a silent witness. The solemn words rolled through me, and I thought of how this would please Deuxième, who had known so little of comfort or kindness. And then Sir Walter pronounced an *Amen* and it was time for us to depart.

Our trio flowed silently upwards. Through dank earth that smelled like Sylvia's garden when she turned it in early spring, through rotting leaves and the moisture of new growth. And then we burst forth into daylight.

We'd emerged in smoke-tainted air beside the corpses of Helga and Sir Walter's Citroën.

I turned my eyes from Helga's burnt skeleton.

Will, Samanthe, called Sir Walter. *If you will wait a few moments, I shall attend to this . . . mess.*

I felt Sir Walter pull away from us, coming solid. Repeating the water-ski maneuver I'd seen Helga doing earlier, Sir Walter scattered graveled earth, putting out the last bits of smoldering-car. Then, using a similar technique, he created a shallow grave and pushed Helga's remains within. A few more moments and the bones and evil dreams of Helga Gottlieb lay buried beneath the graveled earth of Sir Walter's childhood home.

Sir Walter's form wavered to rejoin us invisibly. "*I am afraid that our return journey must be made without the vehicle.*" I could feel something like a sigh of regret pass from his mind to ours. "*As it is but five kilometers, I hope you will not mind.*"

Invisible is working well for me at the moment, wrote Will.

I wondered what would happen when he had to solidify again.

And, Sir Walter? Will continued. *That. Was. Seriously. Badass.*

I felt the rumble of Sir Walter's laugh. *"I believe the two of you are aware of how swiftly it is possible to move in this form,"* he said.

Let's go, wrote Will.

I took a last look around while the wind whispered secrets through chinks in the castle wall. Then I felt the tug of Will's hand within mine, and suddenly we were flying, soaring deliciously along the winding countryside road. A pair of rabbits bounded away from us, terrified. The speed was glorious, and even without the pumping of heart, lungs, and legs, I felt a fierce joy I'd known only from sprinting full-out, holding nothing in reserve. In far fewer than the sixteen minutes, fifty-four seconds it took me to run my best 5K, we arrived at the small cottage.

Will and I rippled back once we were inside the cottage. Mickie, aware of us though she had an arm over her closed eyes, spoke.

"You're back soon," she said. "Was it that boring?" she half-whispered the question to us without opening her eyes as Sir Walter solidified and traipsed down the narrow hall.

"Boring as hell," Will said. He smiled my direction, white-faced, before collapsing onto a sofa across from his sister.

Mick opened her eyes, eyebrows raising in question and then alarm, taking in torn clothing, scratches, and the bloody bandage wrapped around her brother's chest. "Oh my God! Will, what happened? Are you all right?" Mickie froze, temporarily at a loss for words. She inhaled deeply. "Okay. What. Is. Going. On?"

26

WHAT IT MEANT

Sir Walter reappeared from the back rooms, carrying swaths of bandaging. Will, laying upon the sofa, looked like he could use medical attention.

"How do I call 9-1-1 in France?" asked Mickie, her face pale.

"Not necessary," said Sir Walter, setting the assortment of dressings down upon the coffee table. "Nor advisable," he added. "Samantha, if you will, please explain things to *Mademoiselle* Mackenzie. Will and I must leave our physical forms if I am to remove the bullet safely."

With no further word, the pair of them vanished.

"Bullet?" asked Mickie, looking like she might be sick.

I began the tale of all that had happened since we left the cottage. Mickie's color returned as she punctuated my account with salty expletives. Since most of them were directed at Helga, I didn't mind at all.

"I guess *invisible* is pretty much the last word in surgery," said Mickie when I'd finished.

"Oh, yeah," I said, my gaze shifting to the couch across from Mickie, where I assumed Sir Walter was still treating Will.

As I spoke, the air rippled and Will solidified. Sir Walter followed.

"Had to be *you* that took one for the team," Mickie said to her brother, sighing.

Will smiled weakly as Sir Walter carefully re-dressed the wound, binding Will's left arm in place against his chest.

"How do you feel?" I asked.

"Better," said Will, looking dolefully at the restraint upon his arm.

"One fortunate side effect of the timing of Will's vanishing is that the bullet left no exit wound," said Sir Walter. "Had he delayed another millisecond . . ." The French gentleman shrugged.

"At least you got something right there, little bro," said Mickie.

"What did you do to me?" Will asked, looking at Sir Walter. "I feel really . . . well, I feel pretty good compared to back at the castle."

Sir Walter shrugged. "I have had centuries to perfect the art of healing as a chameleon."

"I felt all this tugging kind of stuff going on," said Will. "But nothing hurt. You took the bullet out, didn't you? I think I might have felt that."

The French gentleman nodded. "I knit back together what I could of your damaged flesh. It will be some time before you feel entirely back to normal."

Will's face broke into a broad grin. "You are one talented grandpa."

We spent the remainder of Christmas Day resting beside the fireplace. Sir Walter showed me the woodpile—seasoned wood that burned hot—and I tried my best to care for Mickie's cold and Will's injuries. Our French friend declared he had additional work to do.

"The smoke from the car-fire will have caught someone's attention," he said. "Although, as it is Christmas and my countrymen take their holidays seriously, I think we have a day's reprieve before anyone travels to investigate. Enough time, in short, for me to disguise the true nature of our encounter and activities."

After Sir Walter left, Will told us more. "He's going to bring down the castle."

"What?" I asked, overlapping with Mickie's "How?"

"Well, not the whole castle," Will replied. "But he plans to cover the remains of the car by taking out a wall. He told me while he was doing surgery. I didn't really understand the 'how' all that well. Something to do with rippling back and forth to imitate seismic activity."

"Of course," said Mickie, rolling her eyes.

"Whatever he's doing, it will be thorough," said Will. "He's making sure no one poking around there will leak word back to Geneses about today. Apparently Helmann keeps an eye on the Well of Juno."

"Okay," said Mickie. "I've had my fill of guns and danger. I'm going to bed, and I'm going to pretend my cold is the worst thing that's happened to us today." As she shuffled down the hall she called out. "I will kill anyone who disturbs me before morning."

I piled another log onto the fire, stabbed at the blaze with the poker, building it back to a roaring conflagration. Suddenly I felt aware of Will and our kiss and how we sat alone. My face burned from more than just the combustion upon the grate. I wondered what Will remembered. What he thought.

And I knew it was time to settle this part of my life.

"Will, what did you mean by kissing me back today?"

His features flicked through several emotions. "Um, is this a trick question?"

I kept my expression calm, waiting for his response.

His face flushed a deep red. "Geez, Sam. How many things can a kiss mean?"

"Oh, I don't know. I think I came up with about five last fall. 'I like you,' 'I want you,' 'I wonder what that lip gloss tastes like,' 'I wonder if she'd let me.'" I hesitated then murmured quietly, "I love you."

Will averted his gaze, staring at a lace doily on the coffee table. "So, yeah, all the above except for the lip gloss one. Guys seriously hate that stuff." He ran his good right hand through his hair and closed his eyes as though to focus. "I meant all those things, Sam. Both times. I know you don't feel that way for me. Obviously."

My heart swelled with hope, but the words that spilled out sounded irate. "How would you know that? Ever thought about asking me?"

"That *was* me asking you, last fall." He frowned. "And you answered. You gave me a *peck on the cheek*, like you were my sister or something." His face twisted with aversion.

269

He'd misinterpreted my kiss, the one that meant "I love you, too."

"Not to mention," Will paused, shaking his head. "You *rippled*. You hated it so much you ran off."

"I . . . what?"

His eyes examined the carpet as he murmured, voice soft. "And I'd appreciate it if you found another way to get mad enough to ripple, or whatever that was today."

"I didn't ripple to get away, last fall." I said, my world turning topsy-turvy. "And I didn't kiss you to get myself *mad* enough to ripple today." The idea was ludicrous.

"Well then, what the hell did you run off for the first time I kissed you?" Will asked. "Obviously you didn't *like* it back then. And what was today about? Pity-kiss for the dying boy?" Hurt and anger colored his tone; he wouldn't look at me.

"You—I—you've got everything completely wrong!" My voice had grown loud. How could Will be such an idiot? I dropped to a whisper, suddenly aware of his sister. "I did *not* kiss you out of pity!" The idea was so crazy I didn't even know where to start.

"So you tell *me*," Will said, lowering his voice and meeting my gaze. His brows drew together in a frown; I didn't know what I saw there. Resentment? Confusion? He repeated his demand: "You tell *me* what those kisses meant to you."

270

My throat threatened to squeeze shut. I *hated* the ridiculous tears forming behind my eyes. "I like you," I choked out. "Okay?"

"You do?" Shock washed all other emotions from his face.

"Yes, you dweeb," I said. Somehow I'd crossed the couple of feet between us. I knelt beside Will's couch. I'd left anger and hurt back at the fire, new emotions taking their place. "And I want you."

"Yeah?" A ridiculous grin broke across his face.

I felt like someone who opens their wallet and finds it full of hundred dollar bills.

I leaned in close so that he could hear as I whispered. "And I love you."

"Oh. Wow." When he spoke again, his voice rasped low and husky. "So we should kiss again. To see if I can catch all that correctly this time." His dark eyes bored into mine, hungry.

I ran fingers down the angle of his jaw, stopped my thumb to trace his full lips, leaned to whisper in his ear: "Listen very carefully."

I closed the space between our mouths.

And in that moment I unlearned months of yearning, unlearned the *you can't haves* and the *you shouldn't wants*. Because all I had now was everything. And all I wanted was Will's skin touching mine like this forever.

Heat warmed my belly, spread out through the rest of me like wildfire. And then I noticed the absence of heat from the fireplace; I'd slipped into invisibility.

"Oh," he whispered, re-entering the world minus me. "You blissed out. Like, like . . . staring at Illilouette Creek."

I shimmered back inside my skin, a smile on my face. "Yeah," I said.

"Oh . . . wow." He looked dazed. "You . . . you rippled last fall because you *liked* it when I kissed you."

I nodded, smiling back. "Want me to show you again?" I leaned in to his face, flushed with surprise and happiness, and kissed him. *I like you, I want you, I love you.*

After I'd reappeared a fourth or fifth time, Will reached for my hand instead of my mouth. Pressing his head back into the pillows of the couch, he looked at the ceiling, slowly shaking his head back and forth. His smile grew to a boyish grin.

"I'm so happy, Sam. I just want to . . . I don't know. Punch something!" Here he broke off looking overhead and met my eyes. "You know?"

"Punch something?" I shook my head, laughing. "I have no idea what that means." The comparison involving boys and rocks resurfaced, but I kept it to myself.

His face crinkled with concentration. "No, you know what I mean. Like when you're so full, things just need to explode a little. Like Christmas morning when you're a kid."

I squeezed Will's hand. "I know that feeling." It fluttered warm and joyful in my stomach just now. "It's how I discovered running. When I was little and my grandparents were coming to visit or Mom was making my favorite dinner, I'd feel so full inside. And Mom would send me out to run up and down the block a couple of times."

"Exactly," Will said. "Running right now would be excellent."

"No," I said. "Laying on this couch and recovering from a gunshot wound would be excellent."

Will grunted in annoyance.

I ran my free hand through his thick head of curls. "I've wanted to do that for so long," I murmured.

Will brought my hand down from his hair, turning it palm-forward. Then, he brought my palm to his mouth and kissed it long and slow like I was food he needed to stay alive. A shudder ran through me, but I stayed visible.

He turned his eyes from my hand, resting it upon his chest. A mischievous smile flitted across his face. "I didn't say we had to run *solid*, you know."

27

RUNNING

Before Sir Walter returned, Will and I laid plans to sneak out invisibly in the night to go "running" together. At first, I wasn't at all convinced this was a good idea. It took a lot more kissing, rippling, and solidifying before I agreed. Will was very persuasive.

"Where should we go?" Will asked, idly running his fingers along my forearm.

"Somewhere close," I said. "Carcassonne, maybe?"

Will frowned. "I was thinking somewhere far. You know, see how far we can get."

I shook my head. "Going far is too risky in your condition."

"Come on, Sam. *Risky?* We'll stay invisible the whole time." Will reached his good hand around the back of my head and brought me closer 'til our foreheads touched.

His voice was low, gravelly, teasing. "I'll feel so much better when I ripple. Seriously, I'd have no incentive to come solid." He pulled me in for another long kiss.

I felt my flesh fade away.

"Well, except I can't kiss you when we're invisible," Will admitted, laughing.

I reappeared and sat beside him upon the couch. There was one place I wished I'd been able to share with Will. "At Chenonceau," I began, "The walls must have been almost two feet thick. I passed through one of them when you thought I'd vanished by accident. Staring at the river."

Will slipped an arm around my waist, pulling at me to come closer. I re-seated myself several inches nearer. In the process, I bumped him and his left side pushed uncomfortably into the back of the couch. He winced.

"I'm so sorry!" I said, easing away.

"It's nothing," Will said. But frown-lines still etched his forehead.

"You're a bad liar."

"Of course, when we're kissing, nothing hurts." he said.

I shook my head. But I kissed him, too.

And during that kiss, just before I vanished, Sir Walter rippled solid back inside the cottage.

Smiling, the French gentleman pretended to be preoccupied with warming his hands at the fire. "Does your patient give you trouble, *Mademoiselle Samanthe*?"

Solidifying, I stammered out an answer. "Um, no. He's . . . Will's pretty low-maintenance." I nodded, trying to look matter-of-fact in my assessment.

Sir Walter chuckled. "Some methods of nursing are, alas, beyond my ability to provide."

I flushed. Will grinned. Sir Walter stepped into the adjoining kitchen area.

"Ah, the *cassoulet* has cooked to perfection," said the French gentleman, hoisting a large ceramic casserole from the oven.

I'm ashamed to admit I hadn't noticed the rich aroma—thyme, sausage, something cheesy—until now. I checked my cell for the time: seven o'clock; all was dark although I hadn't noticed the sun setting.

"Dude, that smells amazing," said Will.

"A simple dish of white beans," said Sir Walter. "Meant for our mid-day meal, but perhaps it will do for our Christmas feast. I fear none of us will last until *La Reveille* this midnight."

"Definitely not," said Will, yawning in wide-eyed innocence.

We'd each had thirds by the time Mickie came stumbling down the hall.

"Couldn't be troubled to wake me, I see," she growled in Will's direction.

Neither of us mentioned her threat to kill anyone who'd tried.

Mickie sneezed as she scooped a small bowl for herself. "There's something bugging me," she said, addressing Sir Walter. "According to Sam, Dr. Gottlieb brought two henchman along. What happened to the other one?"

"He sleeps within the mountain," said Sir Walter. "I left him trapped without substance in the hillside."

"He's, like, stuck in the ground?" Will asked. "Buried alive?"

Shudders ran around the room.

"It would be more accurate to say that he is 'buried asleep.'"

Will nodded. "Can he . . . get out?"

Sir Walter shook his head. "Only a chameleon could regain motion and alertness in that state."

"You're sure?" asked Mickie.

The French gentleman nodded. "Anyone else whom I have so placed has always been in the same location when I returned. But I do not plan to return for my cousin's employee anytime soon."

"*Badass*," murmured Will, nodding.

Sir Walter smiled. "I am glad it meets with your approval, my young patient. And now, friends, might I suggest we retire? The day has been long for all of us."

I cleared my throat. "I could stay out here with Will. Since Mickie's sick."

"A most generous offer," said Sir Walter, with no hint of irony. But his eyes twinkled. "Myself, I shall spend the evening clothed in my flesh. I always sleep best in the *campagne*. The 'countryside,'" he added for Mickie's benefit.

Will and I sat silently, me on the couch across from his, as the others traipsed back along the hall.

After the doors clicked shut, Will spoke. "Five hours sleep and then we go running?"

I checked my cell. It was only seven-thirty, but I felt sure I could sleep. I fluffed one of the couch pillows.

"Come here," said Will, turning on his right side and scooting back into his couch.

"I'll hurt you."

Will's mouth broke into a wide smile. "You won't hurt me."

I frowned. The couch looked deeper than a regular couch back home. There might be room.

"I want you close," said Will. "In case I need medical attention."

I laughed. "Yeah, right." But I left my own couch and slowly, carefully, slid myself alongside Will's outstretched form. I felt suddenly awake with his arm holding me close. With his breath warm upon my forehead. With the scent of him—pine and soap and fresh cotton bandages.

But then I began slipping, drifting down and down into slumber, safe and warm.

My cell buzzed at 12:30, waking me.

Will looked alert.

"Trouble sleeping?" I asked.

He shrugged. "Let's just say I'm looking forward to being out-of-body for a while."

"You're hurting."

"It's not that bad. Plus I liked watching your face while you slept. You were deep in some crazy REM sleep just before the alarm went off." Will brushed hair off my forehead. "Bad dreams or good dreams?" he asked.

"Good dreams," I said, smiling.

"Let's ripple," whispered Will.

I started to close my eyes, to focus and calm.

"Not that way," said Will, a hint of a laugh in his voice.

My eyes flew open. *Of course not that way!* I shifted to bring our lips to the same plane.

"Mmmmm," sighed Will, his eyes closing as our lips met.

His lips felt warm but dry, chapped all over.

I pulled back. "You're dehydrated," I said. "Sir Walter said to drink lots."

"I'm . . . what?"

"Your lips are cracked. Just here," I said, touching him softly. "And here." I sat up to grab Will's cup of water. "Drink and then we'll go."

"You're a good care-giver," said Will.

"You're an excellent patient," I murmured as he set the glass down and pulled me back towards him.

"How are my lips now?" He didn't wait for an answer.

Wet, I thought, catching a drip of water tracing down one side of his mouth. *Soft*. I sighed. *Blissful*. I rippled.

I pulled my face back from Will's; our hands held tight together still.

Upon a small sheet of yellow notepad paper, Will wrote: *That's certainly an effective way to help you ripple.*

Quite, I agreed.

Together, we passed silently across the darkened room and through Sir Walter's wooden door.

Oak, I wrote as the delicious smell of one of my home town's common trees washed through us. *Warm, like how it smells in summer back home.*

Yeah, I maybe caught something like that, wrote Will.

Let's go! I typed, suddenly feeling that full-to-bursting sense of joy course through me.

We found the tracks leading north and ran beside them. No. We *flew* alongside the tracks. That's what this effortless glide felt like! No friction, no cold, no aching legs or bursting lungs.

There's a train ahead, I typed. *Let's pass it!*

And as the moon lit our way and the stars wheeled across the heavens, we passed train after train on our northward journey.

The stars must feel like this, wrote Will. *Hurtling through space, you know?*

Leaving the train tracks at Tours, we ran along quiet roads until we saw the tall trees of Château de Chenonceau flanking a moonlit pathway.

I'd love to hold your hand here, wrote Will.

You are holding my hand, dweeb, I typed back.

You know what I mean.

I hesitated only a moment. The nearly full moon crested over the *château*, and I yearned to walk beside Will as well. *Just not for too long,* I wrote back. Slipping my hand from his, I came solid in the chill night air.

"It's cold!" whispered Will, reaching for me.

We crunched along the avenue, the trees like silent sentinels watching over us.

The world around us presented a dozen shades of gray: crisp charcoals, soft pewters, steels, ashes, and silvers. And splattered throughout, the intense white of the moon.

We grew too cold to hold hands, instead pressing our bodies into one another, arms about waists, as we moved towards the castle. *Chenonceau!* Beautiful by day, it appeared by night both elegant and infinitely mysterious.

"Kiss me," Will murmured.

I lifted my face.

"Ready for more adventure?" he asked.

I brought my mouth to his in response.

Invisible once more, we entered the castle. I led Will up to the tiny ante-room.

This is the wall I wanted to show you, I typed, fixing my gaze upon the wall that, on its other side, led into the corridor. *Pay attention to how many different surfaces we move through.*

Silently, we entered the wall.

First, furniture-polish: bees-wax-y and something astringent, like lemons. Then the oak, dry, solid, ancient, a hint of long-ago green. Then stone, Will's favorite. Grains of sand flowing through us, shifting and sifting as we moved through. The scent like riverbank-dirt on a hot summer's day. Then a dry, chalk-y, dusty smell: *plaster,* I thought, and then we were through.

I smelled lemons, wrote Will.

That's all?

Uh, yeah. Was there more? he asked.

We re-traced our path several more times. By the end of it, Will thought maybe he'd caught a whiff of oak.

There's so much more, I wrote. *I'm sorry you can't sense it.*

It's okay. You described it for me beautifully.

We found a clock in one of the rooms that told us it was time to return to Sir Walter's south-of-France cottage.

Sam, I need to talk to you about something.

What?

It's about next week. When we're supposed to go home.

My chest, already invisible, felt suddenly hollow.

Sir Walter thinks Mickie and I should stay here with him.

I didn't type anything back.

I know, he wrote. *Could you—would you—do you think you might stay, too?*

I can't, I typed. The saddest two words I'd ever sent to him.

Yeah. Will fell silent.

There was nothing left to say, so we turned and exited the castle. As we passed through the front door, I thought I could hear the whispered goodbyes of lovers long ago. I paused to listen: it was only the murmur of the wind in the garden.

Retracing our path to Carcassonne, we ran through the night.

The sky shifted to dull grey in the east as I turned his words over and over in my mind. Being apart wouldn't change how we felt. I knew this. Will loved me. I knew this. And I loved him. This, I knew most of all.

The tiny cottage appeared before us, windows dull and dark. We slipped inside. All was quiet. Will's hand fell from mine. In the glow cast by dying embers, I saw him materialize upon the couch. His forehead wrinkled as he re-accustomed himself to the ache of his chest.

I rippled beside him.

"We've got another two days," I said. Two days in a world where Will loved me? It felt infinite. "Rest, now." I tugged at a shawl lying over the back of the couch and settled it across Will.

I sat beside him, holding his good hand until he fell asleep.

Rising, I trailed back to the room Sir Walter had given me. I had a bit of unfinished business hiding in my suitcase between covers of leather. I pushed my clothes around until I found it. Another something I needed to leave behind with Sir Walter. Helga's journal.

Upon returning to the main living area, I found the French gentleman had risen and was preparing strong black coffee and hot chocolate. On the dining table, a brown bag with oily smudges promised fresh croissants.

"Good morning, Sir Walter," I said.

"*Bonjour, Mademoiselle,*" he replied, eyebrows raised as he accepted the book I gave to him.

"It's the one Will and I stole from Helga's office," I explained.

"Indeed," said the Frenchman. He paged through. "*Fascinant!*"

"What?" asked Will, eyes fluttering awake.

"I just gave him Helga's journal," I explained, crossing to sit beside Will. "And you should be sleeping."

"I feel great," said Will. Smiling, he took my hand in his. "Hey, did you hear Sir Walter recovered a flash-drive and two other journals from Helga's car?"

It hadn't occurred to me she'd come by car. But the non-rippler henchman would have made that necessary. "What'd Sir Walter do with her car?"

"Drove it beside the burnt-out Citroën and buried them together," replied Will.

"He couldn't exactly keep it, I suppose," I said.

"*Incroyable*," murmured Sir Walter beside us in the kitchen.

"Sounds like her journal means something to him, anyway," Will said.

"*Mon Dieu, mon Dieu, mon Dieu,*" said Sir Walter.

"Guess so," I agreed.

The French gentleman crossed into our part of the room and busied himself with stoking the fire. "*C'est impossible,*" he mumbled, striking a match.

"*What's impossible?*" Will mouthed the words, looking at me.

I shrugged my shoulders.

When Sir Walter had coaxed a blaze out of the embers and fresh logs, he turned and sat upon the couch opposite Will and me. He blinked several times as though to prevent tears from spilling.

"My dear *Samanthe*," he began. He broke off, however, as if unable to continue. He took a slow breath. "My very dear young lady, might I enquire whether you are still determined upon making the return *voyage* to your home?"

"I have to," I said simply.

"Quite, quite." He looked away, as if to collect thoughts that had fled to the far side of the window. "In that event, might I be allowed to make certain arrangements to ensure your safety?"

My brows pulled together. "Um, sure, I guess."

"Absolutely, yes," said Will, his grip upon my hand tightening uncomfortably.

"Good, good, good," said Sir Walter. "I shall return shortly." Having said this, he rippled.

"What do you suppose he meant by that?" I asked.

Will shrugged. "With Sir Walter? Who knows. Maybe he has a nuclear arsenal at his disposal."

Mickie joined us and together we enjoyed croissants, coffee and hot chocolate. I was clearing off the table when we heard voices outside.

Mickie froze beside her brother. "Don't answer the door," she whispered.

"They're going for the woodpile," I said, recognizing the sound of the creaking door enclosing logs for the fire. I looked through the sheer curtains.

"It's just Sir Walter and some friend," I said.

Mickie crossed to the window beside me. "Wow. A very *buff* friend."

Will chuckled. "Maybe he's hired you a bodyguard, Sam!"

"Very funny," I said.

A moment later, when Sir Walter and the stranger entered carrying logs, Sir Walter began introductions. "*Mesdemoiselles* Mackenzie Baker and Samantha Ruiz, *Monsieur* Will Baker, allow me to introduce *Monsieur Chrétien Sebastien FitzWaldhart de Rochefort.*"

The young man with the long name executed an extremely deep and complex bow. Mickie snorted. Will and I raised our eyebrows in tandem.

28

LONG LOST

"It appears, *Mademoiselle Samanthe*, that my cousin Girard and later his daughter Helga, have been after you for a quite interesting reason." Here, Sir Walter blinked several times. "It would seem that my dear Elisabeth has a descendant yet alive, of whom I have remained in complete ignorance. However, the book that Will and Sam so imprudently removed from Helga's possession has led me to this discovery. My very dear Samantha." Here Sir Walter crossed to me and knelt on one knee, taking my hand. "You are descended in a straight line from my cousin Elisabeth de Rochefort."

I sat, stunned.

"What?" asked Mickie. "Sam's like, your great-granddaughter?"

Sir Walter, now with tears freely streaming down his wrinkled face, laughed. "Well, more like a cousin some twenty times removed. But no less dear than a granddaughter."

I took his hand in mine. "That's why they want me?"

Sir Walter nodded. "I am afraid so."

"That's why my mom died?"

"I am so very sorry, my dear," said Sir Walter.

I nodded. Tears would come later, perhaps. Now I just felt . . . *relief* finally knowing why she'd been targeted.

"And, this is also the reason you must allow me to offer you what protection I can," said Sir Walter, his voice faltering.

My eyes found Chrétien.

"He's your son, isn't he, Sir Walter?" asked Will.

His son? I thought to myself.

"That's my brother," mumbled Mickie. "Pulling crazy ideas out of his—"

"Yes, my friend." Sir Walter's reply cut across Mickie's expletive. "His mother and I never married as you must have deduced."

"Was she Anglo-Norman?" asked Will.

"She was."

Will turned to me and his sister. "When 'fitz' is put before someone's name, it means 'son of,' so FitzWaldhart means Walter's son. Generally a title given when the child was fathered out of wedlock. Back in the day."

"Chrétien," I began. "May I ask how old you are?"

Sir Walter's son drew himself up to his full height of perhaps five feet, ten inches. "I am a man, full-ripe."

Mickie turned her snorting-laughter into a bad cough.

Sir Walter spoke softly. "His birth was in 1638."

"Same as the *Roi-Soleil*," said Will. "Louis the Fourteenth of France."

Chrétien bowed his head in acquiescence.

Sir Walter spoke again. "He would be of great service. Chrétien has generously volunteered to act as your bodyguard."

***

"Your bodyguard?" asked Gwyn, not even attempting to keep her voice low as we shuffled through the Paris/Charles de Gaulle airport.

"*Shhhh!*" I whispered. "He's my cousin, okay?"

"He's my new hot boyfriend, you mean," said Gwyn, checking out his *derrière*. "Will you look at those melons? *Choice!*"

Gwyn kept up a steady stream of remarks like this as we inched forward to check our bags. Beside me, Will held my hand like his life depended on it. Sir

Walter stood to one side with Chrétien and Mickie, deep in conversation.

"So, wait," said Gwyn. "Sir Walter is Will and Mickie's uncle, right? And now he's your uncle too? Aren't you and Will concerned about . . . Well, I mean, that's awkward."

I rolled my eyes and whispered back. "Sir Walter isn't Mick and Will's *real* uncle. And even if he were, there are so many generations between me and Sir Walter that I don't think it would count anymore."

"Okay," said Gwyn. "If you're sure."

"Trust me on this one," I said.

Beside me, Will chuckled quietly.

"Oh. Wait. That means it *would* be wrong if you hooked up with your bodyguard, huh?" asked Gwyn. "So that makes me first in line! Perfect!"

"Please," I replied, tugging at my roller-bag.

We arrived at the airline counter.

"'Ow many of zee bags?" asked a cheerful and elegant *Parisienne*.

"Just one," I said.

Will hoisted it onto the platform.

My bag deposited, it was finally time to say goodbye to Will. My moon and my stars. The person I didn't know how I was going to live without.

"It's just for a little while," he whispered into my ear.

"I know," I said. I pressed against him as if to gather the warmth of his body so that I could carry it all the way back to California.

"I don't know how to say goodbye," he murmured, his breath warm against my ear. "We can't have you disappearing."

My stomach squeezed. I'd forgotten! We wouldn't be able to share one last, lingering kiss. I held him tighter.

"Ah!" he grunted. "Left chest and arm!"

"I'm so sorry," I said, releasing him on that side.

"I'll be fine," he said, smiling, tracing my lips with his forefinger. "We'll say goodbye like the French, shall we?"

"*Au-revoir* you mean?"

"No," Will chuckled. "Well, I mean, that too. But what I really meant is like that—over there." He tilted his head to Sir Walter who was kissing Gwyn farewell on alternate cheeks: one-two-three-four times.

I smiled. "It didn't work to my advantage, the last time I kissed you on the cheek."

Will's mouth pulled into a heartbreakingly beautiful smile. "Ah, but I've learned a thing or two since then."

We kissed one another one-two-three-four times and then a few more.

Chrétien bowed to Will. "Upon mine honor, I shall shield her from harm."

"You do that," said Will. To me, he whispered as he held me once again, "*Au revoir, mon couer.*"

Somewhere in the warmth and sweetness of his breath upon my skin, I found the courage to reply. "'Til we meet again, my love."

THE END

Acknowledgements

I have several people to thank for my twin interests in travel and language which hugely informed the writing of this tale. As a six-year-old, I fell in love with Spanish thanks to my Grandmother, Dorothy Rose, who opened the door into this lifelong fascination. For a bit of help with Chinese, I'm grateful to Lynne Yang. For a lot of French help, I am deeply grateful to Donna Evans, my high school French teacher.

To all my Pampered Chef buddies: you guys rock! Thanks for getting me to France so I could visit Château de Chenonceau, thereby fulfilling a lifelong dream.

My parents, Bill and Adele Rose, made sure I experienced a wide array of language and culture through annual summer trips, and I can never say thanks enough for those travels.

Isabel, Toby, Rachael, and Katie: you are my rockstar beta-readers. I can't imagine taking this writing journey without you! Jacob, thanks for making sure everything looked good, and Ryan, thanks for helping make sure things didn't sound too lame.

Natalie, you make me work harder than I think I want to, and it is always soooo worth it! Lastly, to my husband Chris, thank you for believing in me. What more could anyone ask for?

For information on all releases by Cidney Swanson:
cidneyswanson.com

Made in the USA
Las Vegas, NV
09 November 2022

59030450R00177